I0608300

Social Medium

HEDGEWITCH FOR HIRE – BOOK 2

CHRISTINE POPE

This is a work of fiction. Names, characters, places, and incidents are either the product of the author's imagination or are used fictitiously. Any resemblance to actual events, places, organizations, or persons, whether living or dead, is entirely coincidental.

SOCIAL MEDIUM

Copyright © 2021 by Christine Pope

ISBN: 978-1-946435-41-5

Published by Dark Valentine Press

Cover design by Lou Harper

Ebook formatting by Indie Author Services

All rights reserved. No part of this book may be reproduced in any form or by any electronic or mechanical means, including information storage and retrieval systems—except in the case of brief quotations embodied in critical articles or reviews—without permission in writing from its publisher, Dark Valentine Press.

Getting the Gram

JOSIE WOODROW, GLOBE, ARIZONA'S MOST indefatigable real estate agent and purveyor of local gossip—and the instigator of more schemes, promotional and otherwise, than I could even begin to count—came sailing into my store, brandishing her gleaming iPhone 12 in one hand.

"I have it!" she announced, using the phone to punctuate her words with a flourish.

Although I'd only been living in the tiny Arizona town for a few months, by that point I already knew to be wary when Josie got that glint in her light blue eyes. "Have what?" I asked cautiously.

She waved the phone again. It had a red sequined case that was almost as bright as Josie's short, spiky hair. "I've been racking my brains, trying to come up with some kind of event or attraction that would draw more tourists to the town. Yes, I managed to convince the elders of the San Ramon tribe to hold their poker tournament after all, but I honestly don't think that will be enough to bring the kind of traffic we need."

I'd been in the middle of restocking the rack that held various packets of incense sticks and cones when Josie entered the store. When I first opened Once in a Blue Moon, I honestly hadn't known what to expect in terms of sales, since at first glance, Globe seemed like a very conservative little town, and not the sort of place where a shop that specialized in New Age and pagan books, clothing, and various esoteric supplies would necessarily do very well. And while I had to admit that the books were slower to move, I actually did a fairly brisk business in crystals, jewelry, essential oils, and incense.

Not that any of those sales would have necessarily made me rich…but I didn't need them to. The unexpected inheritance I'd received from Lucien Dumond, late sorcerer and former head of the Greater Los Angeles Necromancer's Guild—GLANG for short—had pretty much guaranteed that I wouldn't have to worry about money for the rest of my life. No, the store had been sort of a vanity project, and so it cheered me to see how many people seemed to truly enjoy shopping there, bringing a little bit of magic into everyone's lives.

Of course, I hadn't kept all of the windfall from Lucien's inheritance for myself. I would have felt positively guilty over being so selfish. No, I'd donated to the fund to build a new gym at the local high school, had written large checks for a variety of food banks and other charities, and had also been fairly lavish in giving to Josie's pet project, the Old Globe Theater Group, which staged several productions each year. Even so, a fairly frightening amount of money remained in my various brokerage and savings accounts. I really had no idea how I'd ever manage to spend even a small percentage of it.

"Do you need me to sponsor another booth at the Fourth of July parade?" I asked, figuring doing so was certainly within my budget. Actually, my budget was big enough that I could probably sponsor the entire parade, the concert in the park afterward, and the fireworks show to follow and not even notice it, but I had a feeling that telling Josie about my seemingly bottomless funds wouldn't be a very good idea. She was already creative enough when it came to inventing ways for other people to spend their money.

She shook her head. "Actually, we're already full up. That's a very good sign, considering we still have two weeks to go. No, I was talking about this. Have you ever heard of Instagram witches?"

And she unlocked her phone and handed it to me.

I took it from her with the same care as someone who'd just been handed a rattlesnake. It wasn't that I was worried about dropping her expensive new phone. No, it was more that the phrase "Instagram witches" sent a worried pulse down my spine. I wanted to dismiss the sensation as a reaction to the mere thought of anything social media–related—I had a Facebook profile because I had a page for the store, and that was it —but my instincts told me the little shiver had probably been my psychic gifts reaching out into the universe and letting me know that Josie was about to bring some pretty crappy juju down on my head.

On the phone's screen was the image of a woman maybe around twenty-nine, my own age. *Almost thirty,* I reminded myself, since my birthday was now only a few days away. She had flamingly red hair the color of a Crayola crayon… a color that didn't even bother to make a nod toward nature, like Josie's bright Titian dye job. The woman in the image on the phone wore a black hood over part of her head, making her hair look that much brighter, and a dizzying assortment of amulets and crystals hung around her pale throat.

"Lilith Black," Josie said as I stared down at her phone. "She's one of the most popular Instagram witches, as far as I can tell. She has two million followers on Instagram and almost that many on her YouTube channel."

"That can't possibly be her real name," I replied, since those numbers didn't really mean much to me and I'd instead latched on to the thing that stuck in my brain first.

Josie lifted an airy hand. "Oh, probably not. But what does it matter? Just think of all the people we would attract if we could get Lilith Black to visit Globe."

Despite the twitchy feeling at the back of my neck, I sent Josie a wry smile. "I don't think we could fit two million people in Globe," I told her.

She lifted an exasperated chin. "Well, of course I don't expect *all* of them to come here. But just think what it would do for our local tourism industry if we could get even a few hundred of her followers to visit!"

For a moment, I didn't say anything, only finished hanging the last of the bags of incense from the display rack. Then I brushed my hands against my jeans—I never bothered to dress up when I was doing inventory—and said, "Don't take this the wrong way, Josie, but why would this Lilith Black even want to visit Globe in the first place? It's not like we're some hotbed of psychic activity."

"Oh, but we *are*," she protested. "Didn't you encounter Lucien Dumond's ghost down by the San Ramon River?"

"Yes," I said calmly. "But that's because he was murdered there. It's not like that particular spot has a history of spirit activity."

"Maybe not," she returned, apparently undeterred. "But I've heard from several people that all the copper ore in the hills around here has its own power. Haven't you felt it?"

I had to confess that I hadn't. Then again, it wasn't as though I'd been reaching out toward it, either. Frankly, the last few months I'd been mostly keeping my head down, trying to ignore the notoriety that Lucien's inheritance had given me…and also trying to pretend that Calvin Standingbear, chief of the San Ramon tribal police, hadn't ghosted me in the worst possible way.

And all right, maybe that was a bit of hyperbole on my part. It wasn't as though he'd disappeared off the face of the planet or something. But right when we were about to go on our first official date, he called to cancel, telling me something had come up and he couldn't make it.

At the time, I hadn't been too worried. He was

the police chief, after all, and I realized he was on call pretty much all the time, even though he had a team of six deputies in his department. But if something important enough popped up, then of course he'd be the one who'd have to drop everything and handle it.

Except he kept making excuses...and then just quietly disappeared out of my life. I tried to ignore the sting of his defection, since it had now been more than six weeks since he'd ghosted me, but it still hurt.

A lot.

The hardest part, though, was trying to pretend as if nothing had happened. Josie had asked a few probing questions before she finally got the hint that I needed her to back off, and although my friend Hazel Marr, a local artist, could tell something had happened...or, more to the point, *hadn't* happened...she'd also figured out pretty quickly that I really didn't want to talk about the situation.

Really, what was there even *to* talk about? So Calvin and I had shared an awesome kiss, a kiss that I'd thought would be a prelude to even more intimacies. Obviously, though, he didn't think our kiss had been a big deal, and so I had to pretend that it wasn't, either.

"I don't know about vibrations from the copper," I told Josie, since she was giving me her patented lifted eyebrow, the one that signaled she could tell I'd wandered off into la-la land again and she didn't appreciate me woolgathering while there was business that needed to be handled. "But I'll try to check it out after I close up the shop today."

"Oh, would you?" she replied, now with an expression of relief. "Because I really think that if you can plan some kind of ritual, something truly spectacular, then you'll definitely put Globe on the map."

"Whoa," I said, and put up a hand, although I knew that sort of gesture was pretty much futile when it came to getting Josie Woodrow to slow down. "I'm not really the 'spectacular ritual' kind of witch. My magic is mostly pretty quiet."

For just a second, she looked almost uncomfortable. I'd gotten the impression on more than one occasion that, while she was just fine with me running a woo-woo shop in her little town and referring to myself as a witch, she still wasn't entirely comfortable with the reality of magic, with the hard fact that it wasn't all just pretty crystals and incense and colored candles.

But because it was Josie, she brushed off her moment of unease fairly quickly. "Well, whatever you can do," she responded in airy tones. "And of course, you'll have to set up an Instagram account."

"I'm not even sure what Instagram is," I protested. "Is it like Facebook?"

That question made her chuckle. "No, of course not," she said. "I mean, I think it's owned by the same company...and I think you post photos and short videos there...and people can like them and respond...but it's still very different."

I had my doubts, but I refrained from commenting. She might not have known the finer points of the differences between Instagram and Facebook, but she still knew worlds more than I did. "I guess I'll pull out my laptop and check it out."

Josie sent me a pitying look. "You don't do Instagram on your *computer*," she said. "It's a phone app."

Great. I'd tried to make sure my phone was just a device for making calls and not a lot more, mostly because I didn't want to turn into one of those people who always had their face buried in a screen and therefore missed most of what was going on around them. But since I'd already promised Josie I'd look into it, I didn't have much of a choice. Besides, it might be a good idea to help spread some positive witchiness out there on the internet. The Goddess only knew the world could use all the good vibes it could get.

"Okay, then I'll download it and install it a little later," I said.

She beamed at me. "Wonderful. And if you have any questions about how to use the app, just give me a call and I'll walk you through the process."

"I will," I promised, although I thought I'd most likely consult Google to try to ferret out the finer points of Instagram and all its particular nuances.

Since Josie had succeeded in roping me into one of her schemes, she didn't seem inclined to linger. She slipped her iPhone into her purse and said, "Well, I'm off. We're doing our first run-through of *Chicago* today." Her hands slid to her hips, and she gave me a reproving look. "I still wish you'd auditioned."

"Josie, I can't sing a note," I replied, which was only the truth. I might have possessed a variety of useful talents, but singing definitely wasn't one of them.

"Still, you would have made a wonderful Velma Kelly."

Somehow I doubted that having someone with the singing voice of a croaking frog as one of the two leads in your musical was a very good idea, no matter how much she might have looked the part. "When it comes to the Old Globe

Theater Group, I think I'd rather be a benefactor behind the scenes," I told her.

At once, she looked almost contrite. "And believe me, it's appreciated. That new seating and the new curtains at the theater are going to make all the difference in the world. And if you ever change your mind about performing—"

"I won't," I said firmly.

"All right." The sparkle was back in her eyes. "Just let me know when you have your Instagram account set up."

I knew better than to argue.

"I will," I said.

Because it was a quiet Thursday at the shop, I went ahead and closed at four-thirty instead of my usual five o'clock. Although the days had been getting longer and longer—and hotter—I still preferred to do my fact-finding about Globe's supposed "vibrations" earlier rather than later, if for no other reason than it would be a way to put off setting up my Instagram account.

My jeans and Keds sneakers would do just fine for wandering around the Arizona countryside, so I didn't bother to head upstairs to my apartment to change. Instead, I went out back to where my

Denim Edition Volkswagen Beetle was parked and got in, wincing a little at the heat that had been baking inside the car for hours. No real point in popping the top, either; when temperatures climbed past ninety-five, as they had today, I wanted to be surrounded by nice, cool A/C, not a hot desert wind.

Even though bodies of flowing water contained their own power, I resolutely ignored going down to the San Ramon River to explore. I doubted there was much chance of running into Lucien Dumond's ghost—after our final conversation, he'd disappeared, never to return, apparently —but I didn't want there to be even the slightest chance of my running into Calvin Standingbear. No, unless another crime had occurred on the banks of the river, he probably wouldn't have any reason to be there, and yet I still thought it better to stay far away.

Instead, I drove to the western edge of town, where there was a nice big stand of trees before the land opened up and climbed toward the Freeport Mine, which was still in operation, although technically outside Globe's town limits. There wasn't a formal parking lot, but a smooth stretch of gravel that seemed to exist for the sole purpose of allowing people to pull off the road and leave their vehicles there so they could go explore the area.

I hadn't stopped here before, although I'd noticed the little spot the few times I was driving out of town, mostly so I could go into Mesa and shop at the places Globe didn't offer—Trader Joe's, Sprouts, HomeGoods. Today I was just glad that no one else seemed to be around, since I always did a better job of picking up vibes when I was by myself.

A breath of hot wind hit my face as soon as I opened the car door, and I tried not to sigh. All right, Globe wasn't nearly as hot as Phoenix, thanks to its elevation, but it could still get pretty toasty. Since I'd spent the six years prior to this on the west side of Los Angeles, where cool ocean breezes moderated the temperature, I knew I was a little spoiled when it came to dealing with hot weather. Supposedly, Arizona would start to get monsoon storms starting at the end of June and that would help to cool things down a bit, but in the meantime, we all had to suffer.

Resigned, I reached in my glove compartment and pulled out the scrunchie I always kept there, figuring I might as well pull my hair away from my face and keep it off the back of my neck. I wore a simple cotton sleeveless blouse, but I still knew I'd be baking once I started wandering around.

However, after I was in amongst the trees—cottonwoods mostly, and some oaks and sycamores and some flimsy-looking specimens I couldn't identify—the air definitely felt cooler. I paused in the shade of a huge oak that was probably twice as old as I was, and closed my eyes and drew in a breath. Almost at once, a feeling of stillness, of quiet, filled me, and I nodded.

This was a good place.

Still with my eyes closed, I spread out my arms and allowed myself to simply be, to let the breeze wash over me, to smell the warm scent of dry grass and sun-baked rock. The trees had a subtler, earthier aroma, one that blended with the other smells all around me.

And yes, there it was—little shimmers of gold and copper and silver, and colors I couldn't even quite name, rising from the earth beneath my feet, filling the air, swirling around me like a metallic fog. All the energy of Globe, all the power that came from the minerals and metals concentrated in the rocky earth.

I could have asked myself why I hadn't felt it before, but that question had a simple enough answer.

It was because I hadn't gone looking for it.

But since I knew it was here now, I also realized that there was plenty of power to tap into. I could definitely put together some sort of picture-perfect ritual for Instagram, even though part of me hated the thought of putting myself on display like that. For me, magic was a personal thing. It would be almost like taking a shower in front of a bunch of strangers.

However, I'd already promised Josie I would do it, so I didn't see how I could back out without disappointing her.

The solstice—and my birthday—was coming up in just five days. That would be the perfect time to put together something show-worthy enough for even Josie Woodward.

Whether I'd could scrape together a big enough Instagram following in the meantime to make it all worth the effort involved was an entirely different proposition. If I only attracted a dozen or so people to the ritual, I doubted that small a number would do much to improve Globe's bottom line.

First things first, though. Since I was in such a lovely spot—and there was a convenient fallen log only a few feet away from where I stood—I figured it seemed the perfect place to embark on this new phase of my career.

I reached into my purse, which I'd slung over my shoulder as I left the car, and got out my phone to check the connection. Two bars. That should be plenty to get started.

Phone in hand, I went over to the log and sat down, then navigated to the App Store and started downloading Instagram.

2

Instant Celebrity

A RUSH OF WELCOME AIR-CONDITIONED AIR greeted me as I opened the door to my apartment, which occupied the space directly over the store. What wasn't quite so welcome was Archie, the cursed cat who'd become my de facto pet, sitting inside the hall and swishing his tail in irritation.

"I'm still a cat, you know," he declared as soon as I shut the door behind me.

"Oh, wow, I would never have guessed," I said, heading into the kitchen so I could pour myself a glass of ice water.

Of course he stalked after me, tail still waving from side to side in a movement I'd come to recognize as his way of expressing his utter dissatisfaction with me. "You said you were going to fix this," he complained. "You said you were going to break the curse."

"I am," I told him as I got a glass down from the cupboard. "I've been working on it."

"Hmph." He was silent for a moment while I poured myself some water from the Brita pitcher in the fridge. "The only thing I've seen you working on is that ridiculous store of yours."

I reminded myself that anyone who'd been stuck in a cat's body for the greater part of sixty years had earned the right to be cranky. As far as I'd been able to tell, it was the late 1940s when a local witch cursed Archie to be a cat after he'd rejected her advances, and the whole time since, he'd been wandering around Globe, just another stray to the uninformed observer.

While I was sensitive to his plight, I also secretly wondered whether my magic was really up to the task of restoring him to his human form. His complaint to the contrary, I truly had been doing my research, trying to find the one spell or charm that might bring him back to himself. So far, it had been slow going. Once or twice, I'd even found myself wishing that Lucien Dumond was still around, if only because he'd been a pretty powerful sorcerer, and maybe he would have been able to come up with a solution, since one continued to elude me.

But Lucien was gone, so I had to go it alone. And it really didn't help that Archie was constantly on my case about the whole situation.

More than once, I'd reflected that the witch in question should've realized he was doing her a massive favor by turning her down. She probably would have hit him with a nasty hex after spending a few weeks in his company.

"You need to back off, or I'll take you to the Humane Society," I warned him.

Since Archie knew those words were an empty threat, he only tilted his head slightly before lifting a paw to give it a thorough licking. "You wouldn't do that," he said in between swipes with his little pink tongue. "You're far too soft-hearted."

No point in arguing with what I knew was the truth. "I ordered some books from a seller in New York," I said. "They're from the collection of a man who had the biggest library of occult works on the East Coast. I'm really hoping I'll be able to find something worthwhile in there."

"I hope so, too," Archie replied. "This is all getting terribly tedious."

"More tedious than when you were stuck wandering around downtown Globe without a home, scrounging from trash cans?" I asked innocently.

He shot me an evil glare and stalked off toward the second bedroom, which I used as an office and was where his bed was located. Not that he seemed to sleep in it much—he always seemed to be underfoot—but I think he liked hanging out in there because I also kept my altar in that room, and he knew he was getting in the way of me performing my rituals. I'd gotten to the point where I could mostly ignore him, true, and yet it still didn't feel quite right to do that sort of thing with an audience.

Let's just say Archie wasn't going to win any awards as Roommate of the Year.

Thinking about my altar made me realize that I definitely didn't want to show off my private ritual space to the world the way most of those witches on Instagram seemed to. I frowned for a moment, pondering the problem, and then realized I had the perfect solution right downstairs. After all, I ran a shop that carried all sorts of supplies for altars. I could just grab the things I needed and set up a secondary altar in the stockroom, a place I could photograph and use for faux rituals, videos I could put on Instagram without ever revealing to anyone who might be watching anything about the place where I did my real work.

After checking that the water in Archie's bowl was still fresh—the cat sometimes annoyed the heck out of me, but I wasn't going to retaliate by neglecting him—I went down the back staircase and into the store. From the locked case by the cash register, I retrieved a boline and an athame, a pair of ritual knives, the boline small and used for cutting paper and other items used in spellwork, the athame larger and showier, used while making an invocation to the Goddess. In addition to the knives, I rounded up a choice selection of crystals, an altar cloth emblazoned with a screen-printed pentacle, and a few more odds and ends. Then it was back to the stockroom, where I cleared off the table I used to pack my occasional mail orders and set out the altar cloth with everything arranged nicely on it.

Once I was done, I thought the setup looked lovely. It wasn't the same as the altar upstairs in my second bedroom, but that was a good thing. I didn't want this altar to look anything like the one I used in real life.

I'd just gotten in a new shipment of manifestation candles, so I arranged several of them on the altar as well, choosing the ones for prosperity and money and health. Even if this was going to be mostly for show, I wanted to make sure I'd be putting good energy out into the universe.

And actually, maybe I needed to watch exactly how much energy I put out there. Right before the store opened back in April, I'd performed a prosperity ritual, figuring I needed all the help I could get when it came to having my store be a success. Not too long after that, Lucien Dumond had been murdered by his younger brother

Eugene and the girl Eugene was involved with, and Lucien had left all his money to me. No one could argue that I was now very, very prosperous…even though obviously, I hadn't been thinking of that sort of outcome when I first performed the ceremony.

Well, there wasn't anything I could do about it now, except try to be doubly cautious in the future.

I'd already set up my Instagram account. Selena_Blue was my username, since I figured I might as well get shout-outs for the store in there while I was doing the more mainstream witchy stuff. Yes, I'd be fine even if the store didn't make a cent, but Once in a Blue Moon was my baby, and I didn't want it to be a dismal failure.

From what I'd been able to tell, most witches on Instagram first posted a photo and a little introduction about themselves to get started. And while my altar was all set up, I knew that I, with my dark, straight hair pulled back in a scrunchie and wearing a plain shirt and jeans—and those lime-green Keds—wasn't anything close to camera-ready.

I went back upstairs and sent a wary look around. To my relief, Archie seemed to be asleep, lying in a pool of sunlight on the living room's polished wood floor. I tiptoed into the bedroom and shut the door—an unnecessary precaution, since the master suite was the one place the cat tried to avoid at all costs.

Even so, I felt better with the door closed.

After that, I went to the closet and got out one of my witchiest-looking tops, the black one with the lace insets and tone-on-tone embroidery. Since it had a low, scooped neckline, it provided the perfect backdrop for me to festoon myself with a bunch of crystal pendants, along with silver pentacles, hands of Hamsa, evil eyes, and anything else that would make me look like an occult practitioner extraordinaire.

I pulled my hair out of its scrunchie, and applied way more eye makeup than I usually wore, accompanied by a dark brick-colored lipstick. Then I stared at my reflection and chuckled.

"Trick or treat," I remarked, and winked at the almost unrecognizable Selena in the mirror, blue eyes circled in kohl, mouth coated in a shade worthy of a silent film star.

Actually, I figured it could only be a good thing that I didn't look anything like myself. Maybe the "Selena_Blue" was a dead giveaway, and yet I had to hope that if any of my former practitioner friends and acquaintances back in L.A. came across one of my photos, they'd just keep scrolling because they wouldn't even realize it was me.

Once I'd deemed myself ready to go, I went back downstairs. The stockroom probably wasn't the most photogenic setting in the world, with its dingy off-white walls and battered wood floors, but with the fake altar positioned behind me, it served well enough.

The photos turned out better than I'd hoped. I chose the one that seemed the best, with me looking suitably sultry and mysterious in front of an altar bedecked with flickering candles, and then did my best to compose a short caption.

Merry meet, my witches! I'm @Selena_Blue, from the magickal town of Globe, Arizona. Follow me for rituals in a place positively charged with magick! #witches #magick #ritual #blessings

Oh, dear Goddess. That sounded absolutely ridiculous. Supposedly hashtags were the way to go, even though it felt as though I was trying to write in a foreign language.

But I'd promised Josie I would do my best, even if the message felt just as artificial as the getup I was wearing.

Before I could lose my nerve, I pushed the screen to post the photo and its accompanying caption. For all I knew, absolutely nothing would come of this. It wasn't as though Instagram—like all social media—wasn't already flooded with millions of different faces and voices, all clamoring to be heard. My silly little post would probably sink to the bottom of that sea of posts, never to be seen again.

I reached for a snuffer—it was never good practice to blow out ritual candles, since you'd be blowing away your intentions at the same time—and was just about to start putting out the altar candles when my phone beeped.

The snuffer dangled from one hand as I bent down to peer at the screen of my iPhone.

It looked like someone had responded to my photo.

Love your look, @Selena_Blue. Can't wait to see more of you and your rituals!

The comment had come from someone named Isis_Moon. Somehow I doubted that was her real name, either. The tiny thumbnail of her showed hair dyed cobalt blue and what looked like the triple moon tattooed across her throat. It seemed she was taking her name—real or not—pretty seriously.

Should I answer her?

I had no idea how this was supposed to work.

Since I was so new to all this, I figured I might as well err on the side of friendliness.

Thanks, @Isis_Moon. I have lots of great things planned!

Another ping from my phone followed immediately. Wow, had she been camped on the photo, just waiting to see if I would respond?

No, this was from someone else, a guy with the handle of Sausalito_Timmy.

Looking good, @Selena_Blue!

Even in his thumbnail, he seemed to be leering at me.

Great. I'd forgotten about attracting the internet creepers along with the people who might be honestly interested in witchcraft. I'd already been missing Calvin Standingbear for a variety of reasons—even if I was angry with him at the same time—but right then, I knew I'd have felt a lot safer knowing I had six foot four of impressive San Ramon Apache ready to glare down any inter-lopers who might decide to show up in Globe so they could see me in person.

Not that I was completely without defenses. I didn't follow the left-hand path, and generally didn't believe in casting jinxes and hexes, but that didn't mean I couldn't send a judicious flat tire someone's way if they got too pushy.

But I was probably borrowing trouble. It was easy to be all creepy on Instagram or Facebook, when you could do or say pretty much whatever you wanted without repercussion. Actually trav-eling to a place to find someone in person required a lot more work.

More and more pings came in, and I realized my hashtags had worked a lot better than I'd planned. Was it normal for the first post of an absolute newbie to garner this much attention?

Somehow, I doubted it. My best guess was that my prosperity spell was working overtime again.

However, I couldn't let my phone keep pinging like that. It would drive me crazy within an hour. Although it took a few false tries, eventually I was able to navigate to my profile settings and turn off any audible notifications.

Once that was done, I realized I was still holding the candle snuffer in my other hand. The thought occurred to me that I might as well take some more photos of the altar, and maybe a video. I could do a quickie prosperity spell, post it in Instagram stories so it would only be available for a short time. At least, I thought that was how it was supposed to work. If the video didn't disappear within twenty-four hours, I could always take it down manually.

I put down the snuffer, then took some more shots of the altar. Afterward, I propped up my phone on one of the stockroom racks so I could leave it recording while I worked my way through my favorite prosperity ritual.

The result wasn't bad, but I could tell I'd need to get better lighting in here if I were going to keep doing these videos on my backup altar. Well, I supposed I could go online and research what would work best without getting in the way of the stockroom's original purpose.

I posted the video with a little disclaimer. *Sorry 4 the lighting! I'm new to this...will get it figured out eventually. #newbie*

Amazingly, I got responses to the video almost right away. New people, too, names I didn't recognize. How the heck were they finding this stuff?

Even more astonishing was the realization that I'd somehow gotten almost five hundred followers in less than ten minutes. Was that a thing?

Apparently, it was...if you were using magic.

I shook my head in bemusement, even as I finally snuffed the candles and uttered a silent thank-you to them and the universe for the energy they'd manifested that afternoon.

Exactly what had I just started?

3

Wine and Sympathy

My friend Hazel stared down at her phone, her expression one of utter shock. "How in the world did you get almost a hundred thousand followers in just twenty-four hours?"

"I don't know!" I replied, knowing I sounded a little wild. And all right, maybe I *did* know…or at least, I suspected. Still, even though I couldn't deny that my spells were pretty effective, never in a blue moon—no pun intended—had I believed I could get that many eyeballs on my tiny little Instagram profile in such a short amount of time. "I mean, I promised Josie I'd do my best, because I knew she wanted the town to get more visitors, but this is just crazy."

Hazel and I were sitting in the living room of the cozy Craftsman-style cottage she called home. Because I'd bought a few of her paintings…and quietly persuaded my mother to buy one as well…Hazel had abandoned her idea of renting out the spare bedroom at her house, since she really didn't need the money at the moment. That change of plans suited me just fine, since it meant we'd have way more privacy for our little chats.

While the house was vintage, its air conditioning was not. We sat in cool comfort, drinking nicely chilled chardonnay as we discussed my predicament. Hazel had come over to my flat plenty of times, but right then, I'd just wanted to get away from the shop and the apartment above it…even while I didn't quite want to admit to myself that part of that desire might have been a wish to be far away just in case any over-eager admirers decided to show up on the property.

"Did you post anything new today?" she asked.

I nodded. Part of me had wanted to delete the app and act as though I'd never started this whole crazy project, but doing so would have been pure cowardice. Instead, I'd posted a close-up picture of my athame and boline—well, the athame and boline I'd borrowed from the shop's inventory—and then followed up with a brief "story" about writing down intentions and burning them in a cauldron. I'd done all that during a short lunch break and hadn't put a lot of thought into it, but even those two posts had been enough to push me past the 100K mark for followers.

"I sort of felt like I had to," I explained. "I mean, here I had all these people following me out of nowhere, and it just seemed like I needed to give them some new content."

Hazel's mouth twisted, although I couldn't exactly tell whether she was holding back a grimace or a smile. The small diamond in her nose twinkled in the sunlight streaming through the windows, although she'd recently abandoned the brightly colored streaks in her hair and left them a soft gold, pretty against her light brown base color.

"And that's the problem right there," she said. "Facebook and Instagram want you to keep posting content for them because that gets more eyeballs on the advertising in everyone's feeds, which is where they make their real money. It's all a huge racket." She paused to sip some chardonnay before adding, "As soon as I figured that out, I deleted both apps from my phone and never looked back."

Wise woman. Unfortunately, my promise to Josie kept me from performing such a maneuver…at least, for now. "I wish it were that simple," I replied.

A shake of her head, and Hazel lifted her glass of chardonnay so she could take another sip. "It is.

You can just tell Josie that this sort of thing isn't for you and that she'll have to go ask the Chamber to put more funds into attracting tourists. Isn't that their job, anyway?"

Supposedly. Globe had a teeny Chamber of Commerce with about twenty members. The organization was presided over by Miriam Jacobsen, a dragon lady in her late fifties who made Josie look like, well, a pussycat. I knew the Chamber coordinated with the City Council on events like the Fourth of July carnival and a Festival of Lights celebration that was held in December, close to Christmas but not too close, but I honestly didn't know what else they actually did. It wasn't as though Globe was exactly swimming in tourists.

"I guess so," I responded. My glass of chardonnay was almost empty, but I thought it would be wise to have a couple of grapes and a bite of cheese off the plate Hazel had set out for us before I poured myself any more wine. "Except I can't really see myself calling up Miriam and telling her the Chamber's dropped the ball when it comes to promoting tourism in Globe."

Those wry words made Hazel laugh outright. "She is pretty scary, isn't she? I remember when she came by the house not long after I moved here and had some paintings for sale in Sundowner Gallery. She knocked on the door and introduced herself, then told me I would be creating the art for next year's Chamber brochure."

"And did you?" I asked. After brushing some cracker crumbs off my fingers, I reached for the bottle of chardonnay in its ceramic chiller and poured myself a half glass.

"Of course I did," Hazel said. It seemed that recollection on its own was enough to require some fortification, because she took the bottle of wine from me once I was done pouring and topped off her own glass. "Can you imagine saying no to Miriam Jacobsen?"

I chuckled. "Not really."

For a moment, we were both silent as we sipped our wine. Then Hazel shot me a sideways glance. "I heard through the grapevine that Chuck Langdon wants to ask you out."

Oh, boy. What was this, junior high? But then I reflected that the gossip channels in a small town like Globe did appear to be remarkably similar to the circuitous routes information had traveled back when I was in eighth grade at Millikan Junior High in Sherman Oaks.

"Well, if he does, he can come and ask me himself," I said after taking another swallow of chardonnay. "He's a big boy—he should be able to manage that without any help."

Hazel's greenish-hued eyes—a perfect reflection of her name—peered at me in some curiosity. "If he did, would you say yes?"

Good question. Chuck Langdon looked exactly like the sort of guy Central Casting would put in the role of small-town hottie. He had light brown hair, blue eyes, and the sort of square jaw not seen since the heyday of 1950s cowboy shows on TV.

Problem was, while I could appreciate his appeal on an intellectual level, I knew he wasn't my type. No, I leaned toward tall, dark, and freaking gorgeous Native American police chiefs.

Even if the aforesaid freaking gorgeous police chief had roundly dumped me on my ass.

"I don't know," I said after a long pause, during which Hazel continued to watch me closely. "At least I know he's not a fortune hunter."

Chuck owned a ranch outside town. Supposedly, he had several hundred head of cattle and did very well for himself. His big Chevy truck was very new—or at least, I guessed it was new. It was certainly shiny enough. Otherwise, he didn't seem to indulge in the outward trappings of wealth; the cowboy boots he always had on looked as though he'd been wearing them for the past ten years, his jeans were faded, and he didn't wear a single ring or watch to flaunt his wealth.

"Maybe," Hazel allowed. "Although I heard his ex-wife took him for a lot of money."

This revelation made me raise an eyebrow. "He doesn't look old enough to have an ex-wife."

She shrugged. "He's thirty-three. I guess they were high school sweethearts, and she dumped him and took off with a plastic surgeon from Scottsdale."

Who I assumed probably made more money than a rancher in Globe. A stab of pity went through me, even though the few times I'd seen Chuck around town, he'd looked relaxed and content, not like someone whose ex had taken him for everything he owned.

Rather than respond directly to Hazel's comment, I said, "It's truly amazing what an encyclopedic knowledge you have of everyone in this town."

That remark got me another laugh. "What else is there to do in Globe except snoop into other people's lives? Not that much 'snooping' is really involved. Josie shares pretty much everyone's business, and if she's not around to do it, there are plenty of volunteers to take up the slack."

"I'm surprised you haven't gone out with Chuck," I said next, then sipped some more chardonnay. "You've been here a lot longer than I have, and you're around the same age."

Her smile slipped a little, and right then, I glimpsed a spike in her aura, a shimmer of pale red at odds with its normal serene blue. No, I didn't see auras all the time—they came and went on their own schedule, as far as I'd been able to tell—but they generally seemed to pop up the most often when someone was experiencing a strong emotion.

So…Hazel had kind of a thing for Chuck Langdon.

I resolved right then and there not to go out with him, even if he asked. My first loyalty was to Hazel, since we'd been friends almost from the moment I came to town. Anyway, while I supposed I might have a sort of exotic appeal, thanks to my gypsyish clothes and dark prettiness, Hazel was just as attractive in her own way, with the sort of friendly, breezy, girl-next-door looks I'd always secretly envied.

"I guess I'm just not on his radar," she said. "Which is fine. I'm not much into dating anyway."

"You've never gone out with anyone the whole time you've lived here?" I asked. After all, she'd lived in Globe for more than seven years. Although I was suffering through my own personal dry spell, I still couldn't quite imagine going that long without any kind of romance in my life.

She shook her head. "No one from around here. I had kind of a long-distance thing going with a guy in Chandler for a while. And I know—

an hour away isn't really that long-distance. But still, the logistics started to get kind of rough, and then he started pressuring me to move in with him…." The words trailed off, and she reached for a grape. Before she popped it in her mouth, she added, "I know Globe is kind of a Podunk town, but it's my town now, and I didn't want to leave. Especially for the Phoenix suburbs."

That last comment was accompanied by a twist of her mouth, showing me exactly what she thought of those suburbs. And I couldn't really blame her. I ventured out that way to do my necessary shopping, but the Phoenix sprawl felt like a vast complex of big-box stores and housing tracts filled with homes that all looked exactly alike. You could probably say the same thing for big chunks of Southern California, although the impression I got from Phoenix wasn't quite the same.

Anyway, I understood Hazel's desire to stay in Globe. I felt pretty much the same way, even though I'd only lived here for a couple of months. There was a lot to be said for a town where everyone knew everyone else, where people didn't feel the need to lock their doors and pretty much the whole town showed up for any special event that might be going on…although I had to admit their attendance at said events probably arose from a need to find something amusing to fill their time. A hotbed of wild nightlife the town definitely was not.

"Well, who needs men anyway?" I asked before sipping some chardonnay.

A knowing glint entered her eyes. She knew all about how Calvin had disappeared on me… and she also knew not to mention it directly. "They're definitely more trouble than they're worth a lot of the time."

We clinked glasses, and went on to discuss other subjects. Even so, I knew in the background, my posts on Instagram were getting more comments, and my tally of followers was continuing to creep up.

And I still didn't know what the heck to do about it.

Sure enough, when I checked my phone after I got back to my place, I'd edged up a little past a hundred and ten thousand followers.

This was getting ridiculous.

Archie emerged from the second bedroom. I could tell from the way his tail was whipping back and forth that he wasn't too happy about me being so late to feed him dinner. However, he took one look at my face and apparently decided it wasn't worth the argument.

And thank the Goddess for that. While it had been good to sit and chat with Hazel, now I was feeling tired and cranky, and just wanted a peaceful evening.

Of course, that was before I made the mistake of looking at the comments on my last post.

I love ur rituals! Are U doing anything special for the solstice?

Globe seems like a magnetic place. What does it offer for the New Age visitor?

Ur smokin' hot. I'd like to—

I deleted that one right away, even as I marveled how social media—and the internet in general—made some people think it was okay to act like complete jackasses when they'd probably never behave that way around someone in real life.

However, the first commenter's words made me remember that I'd planned to do something showy for the solstice. I was thinking a bonfire—as long as I could get approval from Willis Dale, the local fire chief—and maybe some live music. There were probably some kids from the local high school orchestra I could cajole into that sort of activity, especially if I promised them a nice payday for their efforts.

And the second commenter seemed interested in coming to Globe. Josie would like that. Of course, the only true "New Age" activity in the town was shopping in my store, although I supposed I could cobble something together, maybe some kind of vortex tour. No, we weren't in Sedona, but, as I'd discovered, the rocks around here had their own kind of energy. And there might also be the possibility of getting a tour of the San Ramon Apaches' tribal lands, although I wanted to push that idea away as soon as it occurred to me. Anything that involved getting close to Calvin's orbit probably wasn't a good idea.

Still, the solstice celebration idea probably had some legs.

A notion struck me, and I scooped up my phone and headed into the living room. The fireplace had brand-new glass doors, thanks to Brett Woodrow, Josie's nephew and the town's busiest contractor. A few months earlier, Lucien's disciple Violet Clarke had gone crashing through the previous fireplace doors, thanks to Archie launching himself at her head when she tried to attack me, but now everything was put back together again.

However, it wasn't the doors that motivated me, but what was behind them. Since it was way too hot to even contemplate having a fire, I'd gotten a set of faux logs with little carve-outs that allowed you to place tealights inside. It was a fun way to get the flicker of real flames inside the fireplace without any of the heat of an actual fire.

I thought I'd get the tealights going, then do a

short video of their flickering flames, accompanied by a brief caption about a fire ritual on the
solstice. That would be enough to pique some
interest, but because it was an Instagram story, it
would disappear after twenty-four hours.

Five minutes later, the video was posted, and I
felt like I'd been active enough to satisfy my
followers for the evening. Afterward, I settled on
the couch with a bowl of reheated soup and
watched some TV, figuring I'd done my chores for
the day.

For a psychic, I was completely falling down
on the job when it came to envisioning what was
about to come next.

4

Down on the Ranch

"I HAVE THE MOST WONDERFUL NEWS!" JOSIE exclaimed.

Since I wasn't doing inventory that day, I was behind the counter at the store, wearing a black tank top and one of my sparkly black skirts. A couple of customers had come and gone—not bad for a Friday morning—but still, it wasn't as though I'd experienced a mad rush on the place following the video I'd posted the previous evening.

"Yes?" I asked, trying not to sound too guarded. The response to my solstice announcement had seemed oddly muted, and I was now trying to second-guess myself. Maybe I'd only been a one-day flash in the pan, and all those instant followers had already moved on to the new hot thing.

Then again, I'd gained another twenty thousand followers overnight, so it wasn't as though some algorithm had dropped me off a cliff. If that was even how these things worked. I'd be the first to admit that I was pretty hazy when it came to the nuts and bolts that drove social media behind the scenes.

Josie set her purse down on the counter—probably so she'd have full use of both hands. That theory was proved in the next instant, as she waved them in excitement, saying, "I just heard from Mavis Jones—she's the one who owns the Airbnb Lucien Dumond once rented—that Lilith Black has rented the house for all of next week!"

That announcement came from out of the blue. Of course, I hadn't checked Lilith's Instagram feed before I went to sleep, figuring it wasn't as though I could have missed much. Earlier that day, she'd done a live Tarot spread and a small video on writing petitions to the universe…fairly generic stuff.

But it seemed I'd missed some big developments.

"She's coming to Globe?" I asked.

"Yes, for the solstice. She said she wants to tap into the energies here for her ceremony."

Talk about your blatant copycatting. I'd said pretty much the same thing on my own Instagram story. Obviously, she was one of my hundred and fifty-odd thousand followers…or she knew someone who counted themselves among my followers.

I was still very small potatoes compared to Lilith Black, though, and so I couldn't quite understand why she'd be trying to steal some of my thunder.

Unless she was running out of ideas and needed to piggyback off someone else's work.

Apparently nonplussed by my lack of response, Josie went on, "Oh, and I also heard from Leland Price, the manager of the Best Western here in town. He says almost all of his available rooms are booked next week!"

More of my doing? One would have to assume so, since I doubted there was any other reason for there to be a run on hotel rooms in our little town at a time of year that didn't have much to offer otherwise. It was far too soon for the Fourth of July parade—not that the event held much interest for anyone who wasn't a local—and the Festival of Lights, which apparently did attract its fair share of tourists, was more than six months off.

"Did people say why they were coming?" I asked, trying to fight back the sour taste of anxiety that rose in my mouth.

"Why, for your solstice celebration, of course!" she exclaimed. "What else?"

Uh-oh. It seemed like I needed to talk to Willis Dale, the fire chief, sooner rather than later.

"It's tinder-dry around here, ma'am," Willis said, disapproval heavy in his voice. He was a tall, thin man in his late forties, with a receding hairline and a prominent Adam's apple that bobbed in his throat as he spoke. If Josie ever decided to mount a production of *The Legend of Sleepy Hollow*, he'd be a shoe-in to play Ichabod Crane. "Do you really think having a bonfire is a good idea?"

"Maybe it'll rain before then," I replied, the desperation in my voice clear even to me. With Lilith Black and a bunch of other witchy followers about to descend on the town, I needed to have a spectacle to give them. Otherwise, it'd be the Fyre Festival all over again, only without the Caribbean setting…and, I hoped, the lawsuits.

Willis's thin, drooping lips quirked slightly. "It's Arizona in June, ma'am. The monsoons hardly ever start before the Fourth of July weekend."

Since he was a native, he should know. Still, I couldn't allow myself to admit defeat.

"I'll make sure the area is swept clear, that it's only bare dirt—" I began, but he cut me off before I could go any further.

"Sparks can travel miles on the wind, Miss Marx. We can't take that kind of risk." He paused there, and something that might have been a flicker of pity moved in his pale blue eyes. "But maybe you should go ask the Apaches if you can do it over by the river. That's all their land, and so you'd need to get their permission. If you have to have a bonfire, best to do it with a water source nearby."

Oh, sure. I'd just head on over to the complex that housed the tribal government and the tribal police, and ask pretty please if I could borrow a patch of land for a bonfire for a big pagan festival. That would go over really well.

And that was leaving aside the very real possibility of bumping into Calvin Standingbear. So far, we'd been able to avoid each other pretty well, just because we both had stuck to our respective territories. Unfortunately, I doubted my luck would hold if I showed up on his land.

Would he think I'd cooked up the whole plot just as a way to put myself in his path? I wanted to think he wouldn't be that self-centered, but I knew it was a possibility.

Talk about embarrassing.

"I'll think of something," I told Willis. It seemed clear enough to me that he wouldn't budge, and I couldn't even blame him. If our situations had been reversed, I doubted I would have agreed to such a scheme, either.

I left the fire station—and collided with something large and solid blocking my path.

Chuck Langdon, to be precise.

He stared down at me as I stammered an apology, then said, "It's no problem, Selena. But if you don't mind my saying so, you seem a little upset."

I waved a hand, although I had a feeling the gesture didn't appear quite as airy and unconcerned as when Josie did the same thing. "Oh, it's nothing," I told him. "I was just trying to get a permit from Fire Chief Dale for a bonfire next week, and he shot me down."

"That's too bad," Chuck said. His eyes—a fierce, bright blue, nearly the color of the cloudless skies overhead—narrowed slightly. "What did you need a bonfire for?"

"For my solstice celebration," I replied. Everyone in town already knew I was the woo-woo lady, so it wasn't as if I had to hide what I was doing. "But Willis says it's too dangerous."

Chuck rocked back on his well-worn cowboy boots, thumbs hooked in his belt, as he appeared to consider my predicament. "I s'pose it is pretty dry out right now," he said. "But maybe I can help."

"How?" I blurted, before realizing that

replying to his offer in such a manner probably wasn't the most diplomatic way to respond.

To my relief, he didn't seem to take any offense. No, he just gave me a slow, lazy smile, the sort that probably would have had made the hearts of all the eligible women in Globe go pitter-pat.

Mine stayed beating at the same pace, however, probably because of my current distraction.

"Chief Dale only has jurisdiction over activities inside the town limits," Chuck explained. "But you could have the bonfire at my ranch. It's outside the town's boundary line, and it's private property to boot. There's no way he could argue with that."

It sounded like a reasonable offer, even though I wasn't sure whether I wanted to be beholden to Chuck Langdon. If he really had been thinking about asking me out on a date, it would make the situation that much more awkward.

Then again, I didn't have a lot of options. Accepting a favor from Chuck seemed infinitely more appealing than going to the San Ramon tribal headquarters and praying to the gods in every quarter that I wouldn't bump into Calvin Standingbear.

"There could be a lot of people attending," I hedged. "And I don't know what kind of damage they might do to your property." After all, it only seemed fair for Chuck to know what he was getting himself into by extending that sort of offer.

He grinned, a flash of white teeth that was probably very effective in most instances. Only, this wasn't most instances. Despite my best efforts to pretend that kiss with Calvin had never happened, it kept intruding on my thoughts at the worst possible times.

"Tell you what," Chuck said. "How about you come with me to my ranch and take a look at the spot I was thinking of? Then you'll know for sure whether or not it'll work for you."

I probably should have said no. But he was offering to help me out of a tough situation, and besides, Hazel had practically given me her blessing. Not that I planned on anything happening between Chuck Langdon and me, but if it did, it wouldn't be as though I'd be betraying some kind of sisterhood pact or something.

Because the fire station was only a few blocks away from Once in a Blue Moon, I'd walked over, so I couldn't offer the excuse of having to drive my own car. No, we could set out right from here.

Together.

"Sure," I said, figuring I might as well surrender to the universe. After all, that same universe had sent me to Globe in the first place.

And although I'd thought for sure the Lovers card I'd pulled when I was trying to get a read on what I was headed into had meant that Calvin Standingbear was supposed to be the one for me, maybe I'd completely misread the message. Maybe Chuck was The One.

I hoped not; I didn't want to think that the universe would play such a mean trick on Hazel.

"Great," Chuck replied. "My truck's parked just over there."

He pointed to a spot a few yards away. Sure enough, there was his gleaming white Chevy Silverado, chrome accents glittering in the bright sun. I wondered if he washed that thing every day. It seemed awfully clean for a work truck.

But I didn't comment, only followed him over to the truck and then awkwardly pulled myself up into the passenger seat. I wasn't short, but clearly the truck hadn't been designed for anyone wearing a long skirt.

Luckily, I managed to climb in and close the door behind me without incident. Chuck got in as well, even as I wondered if I was making a huge mistake by going off with him. Sure, he'd lived in and around Globe all his life, but if he was a serial murderer, someone should've figured it out by now.

Or maybe not. I could just see Josie on the news, tearfully exclaiming that he'd always seemed like such a nice, quiet person and she couldn't understand why Chuck Langdon, the former high school star quarterback, had a freezer full of chopped-up hikers.

I pushed that unwelcome image out of my head and sneaked a quick sideways glance over at my companion. He had one hand on the steering wheel and his left arm casually propped up on the door sill, and right then, he didn't look as though he had a care in the world. For just a second, I caught a glimpse of his aura, a soothing celadon green with the faintest edging of pale gold.

Nothing threatening there, thank the Goddess.

"Thanks for doing this," I said, since the quiet inside the truck's cab felt a little too oppressive.

"Well, thank me after you've seen the spot I was thinking of," he responded, the corners of his mouth turning up slightly. "It might not be what you had in mind."

Pretty much anything was better than trying to have my solstice celebration on San Ramon Apache land. But since I was the only person who knew I'd been considering such a thing, I decided it was better to keep my mouth shut.

"Oh, I'm sure it will be fine," I managed.

Another silence fell. By that point, we were out of Globe proper and heading west on Highway 60. A couple of miles down the road,

Chuck slowed so he could turn onto a narrow dirt lane guarded by an electronic gate. We didn't come to a complete stop, however, because he pressed the remote clipped to his sun visor and the gate opened before us.

Pretty slick. Then again, he must have come and gone down this road enough times that he had the timing down to a science.

The Silverado bumped along the lane, sending up plumes of dust. I couldn't help remembering when Calvin had brought me to his house, which had been situated along a similar dirt road. Unlike that other lane, this one had oak trees crowding on either side, making for a much greener approach than I'd expected.

This would look great in an Instagram story, I thought, and then was immediately annoyed with myself. I'd been on the platform barely forty-eight hours, and already I was framing my life based on how it would look on someone's phone screen?

Not too long afterward, the lane widened into a large dirt area in front of a series of buildings, including two houses and a large detached garage, along with a barn and a tin-sided structure big enough to house a couple of small planes. To one side of the main house stretched a large pond, complete with several flocks of ducks and geese.

All in all, it was a lot more than I'd been expecting. True, I didn't have much experience with ranches, but for some reason, I'd thought the place would be a lot less impressive.

Chuck parked the truck in front of the garage, although he didn't bother to pull in. "The spot I was thinking of is on the other side of that field," he said, pointing toward a grassy expanse occupied by a couple of bored-looking cows. "I'll show you."

I nodded and climbed out of the truck, all the while hoping that the sandals I wore would be up to the task of hiking through a cow pasture.

Keep an eye out for any land mines, I told myself as I walked along after him, maintaining a wary eye on the ground beneath my feet. Chuck's cowboy boots offered a lot more protection than my own flimsy footwear, although I was glad my sandals were securely strapped around my ankles and probably weren't going anywhere. If I'd been wearing flip-flops, I would've been doomed.

We crossed the pasture and came to a gate on the far side. It opened up into a wooded area thick with more oaks, and also cottonwoods and sycamores and hemlocks. Off in the distance, I thought I could hear water whispering to itself as it moved over a stony riverbed.

I sent a questioning look in Chuck's direction, and he said, "There's a stream that cuts through the property. It's not too full at this time of year, but it does flow year-round. Come on—we're almost there."

He led me in the direction of the water. Before we got to the stream, however, we reached a large clearing with some half-hearted grass growing underfoot.

"I was thinking you could use this spot for your solstice party," he told me. "The trees are back far enough that having a bonfire shouldn't be a problem, and because we're pretty close to the stream, nothing around here is too dry. What do you think?"

I surveyed the clearing. It wasn't terribly large, but I still thought you could fit at least a hundred people there easily. The watching circle of trees made the place feel sheltered and somehow mystical. A solstice bonfire reflecting against the overhanging leaves would be absolutely spectacular on a midsummer night.

"It's great," I replied. "It's such a cozy, sheltered spot." I paused, figuring I might as well point out all the warts before we got too far in our negotiations. "But are you going to be all right with a bunch of strangers tromping through your cow pasture?"

That question only elicited a casual lift of his shoulders. "Oh, I'll move the cows to a different spot. I've got nearly two hundred acres out here, so there's plenty of room for them to range without having to come anywhere close to that pasture."

Two hundred acres. That was a decent size, wasn't it? Considering I'd grown up in a place where lot size was measured in square feet rather than acres, it sure sounded like a big chunk of land.

Maybe there were some other protests I could have conjured. Right then, however, I just wanted to get the matter settled so I knew what was happening and could plan from there. Most of the time, I tried to be pretty loose in my planning, just because I knew the universe was fully capable of lobbing curveballs my way when I was least expecting them. However, this was someone else's property, and Chuck was already being unbelievably accommodating in offering the place for my ritual.

"Then it's perfect," I said. "Thank you so much for doing this for me."

For just a second, his eyes held mine. Even in the shade under the trees, they were almost startlingly blue. I couldn't help contrasting them with Calvin's eyes, which were such a velvety dark brown, they appeared almost black.

The kind of eyes that could hide a whole lot of secrets.

I did my best to banish Calvin Standingbear

from my mind. After all, he'd made his choice clear.

And while I didn't know what Chuck was thinking—I was psychic, but not that kind of psychic—I'd been around long enough to take a pretty decent guess. I got the definite impression that this time around, he wanted someone who was the polar opposite of the cheerleader ex-wife who'd dumped him.

"It's no problem," he said easily, and the tension of the moment before vanished as if it had never been there in the first place. "You're helping to put Globe on the map, so I figure it's my civic duty to give you a hand."

"Still." I paused, then said, "Well, I guess I'd better get back and start planning. It's four days until the solstice, and there are a lot of logistics that need to get figured out in the meantime."

Logistics that I honestly had no idea how I was supposed to handle. I'd never planned anything bigger than a surprise fiftieth birthday party for my mother. While I occasionally attended psychic fairs and New Age conferences, I'd certainly never been involved in the planning stages of those events. It was the sort of thing I normally would have been content to leave for someone else to handle.

But since I'd stuck my foot in it with this one, I knew I'd have to put on my big-girl panties and manage things as best I could, even while I had a sneaking suspicion that Josie would be all too happy to take over the logistics if I asked her to help.

"Sure thing," Chuck said, still in that easygoing way of his. I wondered if he was like that all the time, whether anything ever ruffled his feathers. Maybe not. Despite the cheating ex-wife, it sounded as if everything in his world was pretty well ordered.

We headed back to the truck, and he drove me into town and dropped me off right in front of the shop. As I was stammering my thanks to him once again, he cut me off with a broad smile.

"It's nothing," he said, then paused. "Although I wouldn't mind taking you out to dinner…if you need someone to bounce some ideas off of."

Before I could reply, he put the truck in gear and pulled away from the curb. I watched him go, wondering exactly what I'd just gotten myself into.

5

Lilith Fair

"Oh, so now you're dating the quarterback?" Archie groused as I entered the apartment after Chuck Langdon dropped me off in front of the shop.

I shot him a foul look. Thanks to Chuck's parting comment, I didn't quite know how to handle the situation. It wasn't as if he'd made a specific request to take me out that particular night...or the next. Still, he'd definitely put it out there that he wanted to take me to dinner.

Why did people always have to complicate things?

"I'm not 'dating' anyone," I returned, heading into the kitchen so I could pour myself a glass of iced peppermint tea. My mouth was dry, and although I could have attributed its current state to tromping around the back forty of Chuck Langdon's ranch, I had a feeling the physical exertion that activity required wasn't the real cause. "He's letting me hold my solstice ceremony on his property because the fire chief wouldn't give me a permit to do it in town."

While all this sounded perfectly logical to me, I could tell Archie wasn't convinced. His golden eyes slitted, and he gave one paw a casual swipe with his tongue before saying, "And he's just doing you that favor out of the goodness of his heart?"

"I suppose so," I said. "People do occasionally do nice things for other people, you know."

"Hmph."

That one syllable was all the cat uttered, but his tone indicated that he hadn't been swayed by my argument for the inherent goodness of human nature. Honestly, I couldn't really blame him. If I'd been cursed to be trapped in a cat's body for more than sixty years, I probably would have had a jaundiced view of humanity as well.

I figured I'd better leave it there, just because I knew if I protested too much, Archie would be insufferable if it turned out that Chuck did end up taking me to dinner. The cursed cat was a pain in my rear most of the time anyway; I didn't want to put up with his I-told-you-sos on top of everything else.

"Anyway, I need to get back down to the

shop," I said, which was only the truth. I'd left my trusty "be back at" sign hanging on the front door before I headed down to see Fire Chief Dale, but since it was only two in the afternoon and the shop closed at five, I still had a long afternoon ahead of me.

I hoped it would be quiet. I needed to plan.

Since this announcement was greeted with an expression of utter disinterest—borne out by Archie leaving the room so he could go back to sleep in his bed in the office—I guessed that the matter was closed...at least for the time being.

If Chuck did end up taking me out to dinner, maybe I could request that we meet at the restaurant. Archie was already smug enough on his own; I didn't feel like giving him any additional ammunition.

After smoothing my hair and putting on some fresh lip gloss, I headed downstairs to the shop and removed the sign from the door. No one was loitering around the front of the store, waiting for me to return, so I guessed that I hadn't missed too many customers during the past hour. At another time, that lack might have concerned me—Fridays and Saturdays tended to be my best sales days—but right then, I was just glad of some quiet time in which to work.

Okay, logistics. I got a pen and the notebook I used to make stray notes about inventory and other store-related stuff from the storage space under the cash register and started scribbling. The Best Western had sixty rooms. Double occupancy, that would be around 120 people, give or take. I supposed there was the possibility that additional solstice festival-goers would go slumming and take rooms at the Dew Drop Inn on the other end of town, but not nearly as many. Maybe twenty?

All right, so I figured I should assume a maximum of about 150 solstice attendees. Would that many people fit in the clearing?

I paused for a moment to visualize the space Chuck had shown me. While I'd never been very good at estimating crowd size, we'd had fifty people at my mother's surprise party years ago, and they'd done a pretty good job of filling up the banquet room at a local restaurant that I'd rented for the occasion. That room hadn't been nearly as big as the clearing on Chuck's ranch, so I thought there should easily be enough space for a hundred people. Anything more than that, though, and I'd probably be pushing it.

Before I could get any further with my calculations, Josie came breezing into the store. Judging by the smile on her face, I guessed that she'd already heard about Chuck's and my arrangement. How, exactly, I had no idea, except I'd begun to formulate the theory that she had her own sort of psychic powers, the type that sent feelers out into the air around Globe and sucked up every piece of news and gossip which might be circulating through the town.

"What a perfect solution!" she exclaimed. "Of course Shady Oaks is the perfect place for your solstice celebration! I don't know why I didn't think of it myself."

"I'm sure you would have if I'd asked," I replied, and she gave a modest lift of her shoulders.

"Possibly. Still, it's good to know that you have it handled already." Josie paused there and looked at the notebook on the counter. "Making plans?"

I nodded. "Trying to. I'm worried that more people are going to show up than will fit in the clearing on Chuck's ranch. I need to figure out how to handle that."

She didn't even blink. "Why, sell tickets, of course."

Why hadn't I thought of that?

Probably because I didn't have what you could call a business-y sort of mind. Yes, I was running a store, but Once in a Blue Moon was a labor of love. The place didn't need to turn a profit; it was enough for me to see how happy people were with their purchases, whether it was a chunk of amethyst or bayberry-scented incense or a book on the Mayan pyramids.

"I didn't mention anything about selling

tickets on my Instagram," I said slowly as I turned the idea over in my mind. "Won't people be upset when they find out they have to pay to attend?"

The look Josie gave me was almost pitying. I had no doubt that she thought I was woefully naïve for someone who was about to turn thirty. Still, she didn't miss a beat as she replied, "Then don't *sell* them. Just tell people they have to come into the shop to get a free ticket, and once the tickets are gone, they're gone. That way, you aren't charging people to go to your solstice ritual, but you're still getting them to come to your store. With any luck, most of them will buy something while they're here."

Once again, I had to wonder why I hadn't thought of such a solution. It seemed like the perfect way to handle the ticket distribution without getting anyone too angry. And, as Josie had pointed out, if people did a little shopping while they were in the store, it would be a win-win for everyone.

"I think that's a great idea," I told her, and was glad to see her beam at the praise. "I'll get some tickets printed up and then put the announcement on my Instagram."

"Go see Dave at Golden Globe Printers," she said at once. "He's the best in town—and he'll have them done for you quickly. He can also do the graphics if you don't want to do them yourself."

That also sounded like a wonderful solution, since about the best I could manage when it came to graphic design was cobbling together a very basic flyer in Microsoft Word using supplied images. I supposed I could have asked Hazel to help out, although honestly, I didn't know how much graphic design experience she even had. Painting in oils wasn't exactly the same thing as designing a ticket or a brochure.

"Will do," I said. "Thanks for the reference."

One of Josie's patented hand waves. "Oh, I just want to make sure this whole affair runs as smoothly as possible. After all, this will be the first taste of Globe for most of these people." She paused there, brow furrowing for a second or two as she appeared to think things over. "I suppose I should let all the restaurant owners know that there's going to be a large crowd of people coming in from out of town next week, and to be ready."

"Isn't that the sort of thing Miriam Jacobsen should be doing?"

A flicker of dislike moved over Josie's features, come and gone so quickly, I wondered if I'd imagined it. Then again, I could see why the two women wouldn't want to have much to do with each other. It would be like the irresistible force meeting the immovable object. "Oh, she's busy with other things. I don't mind getting the word out." She reached across the counter and patted me on the arm. "You just have Dave print up the tickets, and make whatever kind of announcement you need to. We can take care of the rest."

Having delivered those reassuring words, she turned and went sailing out the door. It closed behind her with a little jangle of the bells I had hanging from it, and I smiled to myself.

I should have known Josie would step in and take over. Not everything, of course; I knew she had no desire to learn anything about the actual ritual I'd be performing, and in fact would try to keep her distance from certain aspects of my practice in general, but for the boots on the ground stuff, she wanted to be in control.

Which was fine by me. Everyone had their particular areas of expertise, and planning wasn't one of mine. Otherwise, I probably would have gone into an entirely different field of work.

I flipped to a new page in my notebook, figuring I should jot down some basic instructions for the tickets to the solstice festival. Date and place and time, obviously…and probably directions on the reverse side, since Shady Oaks Ranch wasn't exactly the easiest place in the world to find, especially if you'd never been in this part of the world before. Maybe I could have Dave the printer find some kind of simple line art with a sun and moon, something to show the reason for the festival.

The bells on the shop door jingled again, and I looked up, thinking that maybe Josie had thought of something she'd forgotten and had returned to tell me about her latest insights, or possibly Chuck had decided to stop by and really ask me out to dinner, rather than hinting his way around the topic.

Or it could be a customer, of course.

However, as soon as I looked at the woman who'd entered the shop and paused to glance around, I knew exactly who my new visitor was.

Lilith Black, Instagram witch.

In person, her hair seemed even more Crayola-bright, or maybe that was because of the pallor of her skin and the fact that she was dressed in black from head to toe. The same amulets and crystals she wore in her profile photo hung around her neck, and a slender silver ring gleamed in her patrician nose.

Entering the shop immediately behind her were a man and a woman. I guessed the man was probably around my age or a little older, in his middle thirties at the most. He looked like the kind of goth guy who'd be hanging around with someone named Lilith Black—he also wore all black, and silver hung from multiple piercings in his ears, while elaborate tats showed beneath the rolled-up sleeves of his black dress shirt. His hair was black, too, ragged and shoulder-length, like Severus Snape had been his hairstyle inspiration.

The woman who accompanied them appeared to be a lot younger, probably in her early twenties. She had brown hair pulled back into a tight pony-tail and wore a prim little black dress with a white collar, black tights, and black Mary Jane–style shoes. If Professor Snape had been the guy's style inspiration, it looked like their companion wanted to be Wednesday Addams when she grew up.

The trio advanced toward the counter where I stood, with Lilith Black in the lead. As she drew closer, I realized she was probably a few years older than I; faint lines around her eyes and etched from her nose to her mouth were revealed up close that would have been blurred by the filters she used on Instagram. Still, no one could deny the elegant angles of her face, the sort of bone structure that would hold up through the years.

She paused directly in front of me, her companions stopping almost a precise foot behind her. I wondered if they practiced that maneuver in private.

"Hello," I said, figuring I might as well act the part of the cheery shopkeeper, even though I knew exactly who my visitors were. Or rather, I knew who Lilith Black was—the other two were obviously her assistants...or lackeys. "Welcome to Once in a Blue Moon. Can I help you find something?"

"I am Lilith Black," she said, in the same sort of tone I would've expected someone to announce they were the Queen of England. It was also the kind of tone that seemed to imply she expected me to have heard of her.

Well, with more than two million followers, she was probably well known in most witchy circles. Still, I wasn't sure how to respond. Saying I was a big fan seemed kind of disingenuous, considering I hadn't even known who she was until a few days earlier.

But because pretending total ignorance also didn't seem like a good idea, I decided to attempt a neutral middle ground. "Oh, hi," I responded, knowing the words sounded limp at best. "I saw on Instagram that you were planning to come to Globe. Welcome to town—I'm Selena Marx."

Her cool gray eyes surveyed me for a moment, as if to say, *I know who you are.* Instead, she remarked, "You're the witch Lucien Dumond left all his money to, aren't you?"

Talk about cutting to the chase. Was that why she'd come to Globe, to ask me for money?

Even as the thought flitted through my mind, I dismissed it as completely ridiculous. I didn't have the faintest idea how Instagram witches and

YouTubers made their money, but even I knew that someone who had her numbers of followers probably wasn't hurting for cash.

I didn't bother to ask how she knew about my unexpected inheritance. Although I'd kept tight-lipped about the whole thing—on the advice of my lawyers—I knew that the surviving members of GLANG had probably spread the story around enough that anyone within certain circles in the occult community must have heard about what had happened.

"He left me some," I hedged, which wasn't a complete lie. A very small percentage of Lucien's fortune had gone to his parents and his brother Eugene. Of course, now that Eugene was a perma-nent resident of the maximum-security prison in Florence, Arizona—or at least permanent for the next twenty-five to thirty years—he couldn't exactly spend any of that money. I wondered what had happened to it. "And I've donated a lot to local charities."

"How kind of you," Lilith said, in a tone that seemed to indicate she thought my actions were anything but. Before I could respond, she went on, "I just thought I'd drop in and let you know I was in town—as a professional courtesy."

"Well, thanks," I replied, since I didn't know quite what else to say. Her entire attitude told me that she didn't think me much of a threat...not that I would have even been inclined to look at the situation in such a way. Witches generally were cooperative, not competitive, and so I was a little mystified by her subtly veiled hostility.

A pause as she took another glance around the shop. For just a second, I caught glints of yellow spiking in her aura, telling me she was a little envious of the place, had probably hoped that it would be a dump so she could feel superior to me in yet another way.

Sorry, sweetheart, I thought. *I put a lot of work into this shop. It may be tucked away in Globe, Arizona, but it's not some cut-rate discount store.*

Apparently ignoring my thank-you, she added, "I also wanted to let you know that I'll be hosting my own solstice ritual here. I've done some exploring around town, and the energies in Globe are perfect. I know you have a ceremony of your own planned, but I don't want you to get too upset if I draw some of your celebrants to my ritual."

I supposed I should have expected as much. It took a lot of effort to keep myself from glancing down at the notebook that held all my scribbled calculations about the ceremony I was planning at Chuck's ranch. Best guess, I probably wouldn't need to be too worried about capacity at the clearing down by the stream. With my luck, I'd have to start scrounging up people to attend.

"That's fine," I said, my tone as even as I could make it. The last thing I wanted was for her to get under my skin. "I didn't want anything too large anyway. If a ritual gets too big, then it loses all the power of its intimacy."

For just a second, her nostrils flared in annoyance. Good. It had been a subtle barb, but I'd still wanted it to draw a little blood.

"Small and intimate is probably best for a beginner witch," she replied with a lift of her chin.

Of all the—

"Oh, I'm not a beginner," I said sweetly. "I'm new to social media, but I've been practicing since I was nineteen years old."

"So, for more than ten years?" she asked, and I had to resist the impulse to ask her the age on her driver's license. I might have been a few days away from turning thirty, but I still got carded on a regular basis.

"Long enough," I replied, almost preternaturally calm. I absolutely would *not* let her mean girl schtick get to me.

"Good," Lilith said. "Because I'm always concerned when an inexperienced practitioner attempts a ritual that's too advanced for her. Those things never turn out well."

About all I could do was nod. Behind her, the

Wednesday Addams lookalike had observed the whole exchange with absolutely no shift in her expression. The Snape impersonator, on the other hand, had just the faintest quirk to his mouth, one that told me he found the situation secretly amusing.

Great. I'm so glad I could be here to entertain you.

Before I could say anything else, Lilith added, "Oh, just so you know, I'll be performing my ritual by the river, over on the San Ramon Apaches' land. I reached out to the tribal elders to get permission earlier today, and they were so kind about it. I'm surprised you didn't try to have your ceremony there—it really is the perfect spot."

Having delivered that tidbit, she sent me an insincere smile and then turned, striding back toward the door with the smugly confident air of someone who'd just skewered their opponent in a fencing match. Her two companions followed, although Snape gave me just the slightest over-the-shoulder glance before he headed outside.

Was that pity in his expression?

Maybe. I wasn't in the correct mental state to analyze his reactions. Instead, I was boiling inside.

How dare she?

Never mind that I didn't have any more claim to San Ramon Apache land than I did the Holy Roman Empire. And all right, if I really stopped to analyze my feelings—something I'd trained myself to do ever since I started doing readings professionally, since you couldn't really going around charging other people for spiritual advice unless you had your own house in order—I knew a big part of the anger that churned inside me right then was merely jealousy.

And that was ridiculous, because it wasn't as though Lilith had announced she was performing a sex ritual with Calvin Standingbear on the banks of the San Ramon River. No, she'd done what I should have done, if I weren't being such a coward about the whole thing. She'd merely reached out to the tribal elders for permission, and they'd given it…for whatever reason.

Still, I was angry, mostly because I knew she'd only showed up in Globe to steal my thunder. It was her way of marking her territory, of letting me know that some upstart from the wilds of Arizona wasn't going to horn in on her Instagram action.

Fine. I'd never been a competitive person—my philosophy had always been "do as you will as long as it does no harm"—but something about that woman had gotten my hackles up. And Lilith Black might have had millions of followers on her side, but I had one thing she didn't.

The people of Globe.

Yes, I was still new in town, but I owned a business here, had already done a lot for the community in terms of donations to various worthy causes. Some of my fellow townspeople might not have completely understood my witchiness, and yet I was still one of them now. I had to believe they'd be on my side.

Either way, this was war.

6

Dinner for Two

OBVIOUSLY, I WASN'T GOING TO LET THE world know that things weren't entirely sunny in Globe, Arizona. I supposed that was one of the good things about social media—you could show only what you wanted people to see and hide the rest.

So I posted about the ticket situation, and let my followers know they'd be able to pick up their tickets at the shop on Monday. That didn't leave a whole lot of time, since the solstice celebration would be on Tuesday evening, but Dan had told me Monday morning would be the soonest he'd have the printed tickets ready. The Instagram post got some reactions…although not nearly as many as I'd been expecting.

Had Lilith's rival solstice ritual already siphoned off a bunch of my attendees?

If so, there didn't seem to be much I could do about it, except fume inwardly. My Gemini sun and Libra moon made me practically allergic to confrontations, so even though having fewer people attend my ritual might be a blow to my ego, I knew I didn't have the intestinal fortitude to get in Lilith Black's face about her skullduggery. At any rate, did it really matter whose ritual people attended, as long as they came to town and spent some of those lovely tourist dollars in Globe?

Just as I was about to lock up and head upstairs to my apartment for a much-needed glass of wine, Chuck Langdon entered the shop. The cowboy hat was gone, but otherwise, he still wore the same faded Levi's, worn-out cowboy boots, and plaid shirt he'd had on earlier in the day.

"Oh, hi," I said, a little surprised. I suppose I'd assumed that if he wanted to get in touch, he would've just called or texted.

"I saw your Instagram post," he said, and I blinked at him.

"You're on Instagram?"

A slow, lazy smile spread across his lips. It was the sort of smile that probably made a lot of the women around town weak in the knees, but I found myself curiously immune to its charms.

"I am now."

As I was wondering how to reply to that comment, he continued.

"Doing anything for dinner tonight?"

Unless eating leftover gazpacho counted as "anything," I really wasn't. But I was tired and cranky after that visit from Lilith Black and her lackeys, and I didn't think I was in the right mood to be the level of charming required for a first date.

If that's even what this "dinner" was supposed to be.

"Um…." I hedged. After Chuck had been so nice to me, it seemed downright rotten to answer "no" to his question. On the other hand, he probably deserved better than to be inflicted with my bad mood.

Still smiling, he came a bit closer to the counter. "You're under no obligation to say yes. My offer to use the ranch for your ritual still stands."

Dammit, did he have to be so nice? It would be a lot easier to blow off someone who was a jerk.

"I've had a craptastic day," I blurted. "I'm not sure I'd be very good company."

"Sorry to hear that," he said, his tone easy. "But why don't you let me buy you dinner? You can tell me all about your crappy day over a steak and a bottle of cabernet."

That actually sounded heavenly. But….

"Where in Globe can you get a steak dinner and a bottle of wine?"

He chuckled. "Okay, you got me. You can't... I'd have to take you to the restaurant over at the casino outside town."

Oh, that really didn't sound like a good idea. What if Calvin saw me out on a date with Chuck Langdon?

So what if he does? I scolded myself. *Are you going to completely nuke any chance at having a personal life because you won't stop mooning over someone who doesn't even want you?*

When I put it that way....

"That would be great," I said, making sure my tone was firm enough that I had no chance of backing out. "I've never been there."

"Then that's where we'll go. I need to run home and change. Pick you up at seven o'clock?"

"Sure."

"See you then."

He nodded at me and went back out. I watched him go, and wondered if I'd just made a colossal mistake.

Chuck had given me enough time to check in on Lilith's feed, since I didn't really have to change my own outfit, only freshen my makeup and run a brush through my hair. And while I was still beyond annoyed with Ms. Instagram Supreme, I figured I needed to see what she was up to, if only so I'd have some sort of counter-measures in place in case she decided to go on the offensive.

She'd posted a couple of videos, one showing off the Airbnb where she was staying—pettily, I hoped the owner of the vacation rental hadn't bothered to smudge the place or do anything else to cleanse the place of the negative vibes Lucien and his murderer Violet had left behind—and another in which she'd gone with her two lackeys to survey the spot where she planned to hold her ritual.

I'm sure it was mere coincidence that led her to choose the exact place where Lucien Dumond had died.

Logically, it made sense. The large clearing that opened onto an expanse of rocky riverbank provided enough room for plenty of observers to congregate and observe Lilith's ritual. Probably more than would fit in my designated area on Chuck's ranch, even though I tried to remind myself this wasn't a competition.

Right.

Also, with the running water only a few feet away, and the ritual fire I was sure she had planned, she would be able to combine all four elements of her ceremony with everything the setting itself had already provided.

All in all, it did seem like an ideal place for her to work. Problem was, a man had died violently there only two months earlier. I knew Lucien's spirit was long gone—I'd had one last convo with him before he moved on from this plane—and yet even if his ghost wasn't an issue, the psychic residue of that kind of violence could linger in a spot for a very long time.

And that meant the place would really need to be thoroughly cleansed before it could be deemed safe for any kind of magical working.

I tried to tell myself that Lilith wasn't an amateur, and so of course she'd make sure the clearing was swept clean of any other energies. For all I knew, the tribal elders had informed her that a crime had taken place there, and that it was probably a good idea to choose another location. From what I'd seen of Lilith Black so far, however, I'd gotten the impression she wouldn't listen to their warnings. If she'd decided the clearing was the place to be, then that was where the ritual would happen.

Which meant there probably wasn't any point in me trying to issue my own warnings. If she wasn't going to listen to the tribal elders, then she sure wasn't going to listen to me. Any prophesies of doom coming from my lips would be viewed as a transparent ploy to get her to use a less picturesque location for her ceremony.

The buzzer for the back entrance to the building sounded then. I glanced at the clock. Exactly seven.

I had to admit that I liked a man who was on time. My Neptune in Capricorn asserting itself, probably.

Archie, who'd been fed an hour earlier and was lying on the rug in the entryway, shot me a baleful glance. "So much for not dating the quarterback," he remarked.

"Isn't there a statute of limitations on how long being the high school quarterback is a determining influence in your life?" I shot back. "I mean, the guy is in his early thirties."

"So you admit you're going out with him."

"We're going to dinner," I said. "That's all."

"Hmph."

And then Archie stalked off toward the living room and jumped up on an arm of the sofa. He knew I didn't like him getting on the furniture… which of course was exactly why he'd done it.

Because Chuck was waiting downstairs, I didn't have time to get into an argument. No, I just grabbed my purse from where it had been sitting on the hall table, then engaged the alarm system before I let myself out and locked the door behind me.

Most likely, the security system was overkill, but I felt better knowing it was there.

As I hurried down the stairs, I wondered what the heck had put Archie's nose out of joint. After all, why should a cursed cat who'd formerly been an asexual man care who I was going out with? He couldn't be *jealous,* could he?

I decided that theory was way too self-serving. While I could look in the mirror and determine in an objective way that I was pretty, I certainly had never been one of those women who thought that every man—even a man in a cat's body—was dying of love for me.

"Sorry," I said breathlessly as I emerged on the back stoop and saw Chuck waiting there. "I had to get everything locked up and the alarm system turned on."

One eyebrow lifted. He'd exchanged the faded work shirt for a crisp button-up in a nice shade of teal, and his jeans looked newer, but those scuffed cowboy boots were still on his feet. I couldn't help wondering if he wore them to bed.

Not that I had any intention of finding out.

"You expecting a crime wave?"

I managed a not very convincing chuckle. "No, but I'm from L.A. Old habits die hard."

He seemed to accept that explanation, because he nodded and said, "Ready to get going?"

"Sure," I replied, trying to ignore the butterflies in my stomach. It wasn't nerves about going on a dinner date with Chuck Langdon as much as my worry that we might bump into Calvin at the casino's restaurant. Even though I'd tried to tell myself I was fretting over something that probably wouldn't even happen—nothing Calvin had said or done had made me think he ever visited the casino, except in a professional capacity—I couldn't quite ignore the sensation of impending doom that had been hovering in my mind ever since Chuck had told me where we would be going for dinner. In most instances, such a sensation was something that could be dismissed as anxiety and nothing else, but when you were psychic, you ignored those feelings at your peril.

However, I couldn't back out now. I tried to seem as calm as possible as Chuck opened the truck's door for me, then waited until I was safely in the passenger seat before he closed the door and went around to his side of the vehicle.

Quite gentlemanly, actually. It wasn't the sort of courtesy I'd gotten from the men I'd dated back in Los Angeles, but it seemed that in Globe, people were still raised with old-fashioned manners.

Mostly, I thought, recalling my brusque treatment at Chief Henry Lewis's hands, although I supposed his rudeness had mostly stemmed from irritation at my butting into the investigation of

Lucien Dumond's death. Even though I'd been instrumental in outing Lucien's murderers, Globe's top cop still wasn't too thrilled with me.

Chuck cut down to Highway 60 and followed it eastward out of town. Neither of us spoke at first, and I racked my brain for an innocuous topic of conversation.

"Do the monsoons really not start until after the beginning of July?" I asked, apropos of nothing, and he sent me a sideways look.

"Depends," he replied. To my relief, his tone sounded natural enough. "That's the traditional start, I suppose, but some years it's later and some years it's earlier. We've had a couple of pretty dry seasons in a row, so we're all hoping it'll change with this go-'round."

No wonder Willis Dale had been worried about fires. And I had to admit that the hillsides outside Globe had looked sort of parched, but since I was still getting used to the terrain around here, I'd just assumed Arizona was always that dry.

"Maybe I should do a rain dance instead of a solstice ritual," I joked, and once again Chuck gave me a sidelong glance.

"Can you do that?" he asked, sounding genuinely curious.

"Well, it's not like a Native American ceremony or anything," I said. "But there are rituals for the weather, just like there are for everything else. I'll admit that weather magic isn't my field of expertise, though."

The corner of his mouth that I could see lifted slightly. "Then we should probably just leave it to Mother Nature for now. If things start looking dire in mid-July, maybe we'll have to ask you for help."

That suggestion sounded reasonable enough to me. Weather magic could be tricky, and, like I'd told him, it wasn't something I had a lot of experience with. "Sounds like a plan."

We settled back into silence after that, but it was a more companionable one, not nearly as awkward as when we'd first pulled away from my building. Globe had already slipped behind us, and the world felt vast and dark. I usually was safely at home when night fell, so heading east on the highway, it really hit me how vast and black the countryside was out here, unrelieved by a single street lamp or house with its lights on. Brilliant stars shimmered overhead.

Coming into view, however, was an oasis of light that proved to be the Gold Dust Casino. It was nowhere near as big as the single Native American casino I'd visited—Pechanga just outside Palm Springs—but it looked respectable enough, with a row of palm trees out front and stacked rock surrounding its plate glass front doors.

The lot was more crowded than I'd expected, and so we had to park a good ways off. Since I wore flat sandals, the walk wasn't a big deal, although the night air was warm enough that the air conditioning inside the casino felt wonderful after traversing the parking lot.

It seemed Chuck had made reservations, because we were ushered into the restaurant without having to wait at all. More stacked rock composed the walls, and the colors were warm and subdued and utterly Southwest—soft coral, warm sand, dusty turquoise.

The hostess, a pretty girl with long black hair, obviously one of the San Ramon Apache, took us to a quiet booth off to one side. While I appreciated the privacy—I'd never liked being stuck at a table out in the middle of the restaurant floor—I uneasily wondered if Chuck had requested a spot like this because it was much more romantic.

But I tried to seem natural as I slid into the booth and took the menu the hostess handed me. To my relief, Chuck didn't try to sit too close, but settled himself a respectable foot or so away.

"Everything's good here," he said, "so if you're not a red meat kind of person, you don't have to order steak. It was just a suggestion."

Red meat was an indulgence for me, true; I usually had it once or twice a month, if even that much. Since I'd been good lately, I figured it couldn't hurt to order it tonight. Besides, if we both got some kind of steak, choosing a wine would be easier.

"No, steak sounds great," I told him. "I haven't had one in months."

He looked a little relieved at that statement. Maybe he'd been worried about the wine selection, too.

When our waiter came by—a good-looking man with high, sharp cheekbones, black hair pulled back into a ponytail—Chuck asked for a bottle of cabernet, and we both placed our orders. Once that was done, another of those awkward little silences fell.

Obviously, he thought it was his duty to initiate the conversation this time, because he reached for his glass of water as he said, "So, how did someone like you ever end up in Globe, Arizona?"

I chose to take the "someone like you" comment as a compliment. "You mean Josie hasn't spread the story far and wide?"

He grinned, showing off friendly crinkles around his bright blue eyes. Oh, yes, definitely cute. I knew my mother would be ecstatic if I hooked up with someone like Chuck Langford.

But since I'd never run my personal life to please my mother...or anyone other than myself...I wasn't going to let that internal observation sway me.

"I don't have much time to listen to Josie Woodrow's gossip," he said. "The ranch keeps me pretty busy."

"Ah," I said, wondering if he handled all of the livestock on Shady Oaks Ranch himself. That didn't seem very likely, though, and I filed the question away for further on in our conversation. "Honestly, it was about the psychic equivalent of sticking a pin in a map and seeing where I was headed. Or maybe not exactly like that—the universe gave me some pretty clear signals as to where it wanted me to go."

Chuck absorbed that confession in silence. Was he thinking I sounded like a complete whackadoodle? I suppose to the uninitiated, accepting signals from the universe did seem pretty out there.

But my experience had taught me that the universe really did its best to let us know what it wanted for us. If we were too busy or preoccupied or just downright dense to acknowledge those signals, well, whose fault was that?

His smile widened, though, and he said, "Well, then, I guess I should thank the universe for sending you here."

Oh, dear. I was saved from having to make a reply by the arrival of our waiter with the bottle of cabernet. Once he'd opened the bottle and poured us each some wine—and assured us that our salads would be out shortly—the awkwardness of the moment had passed, thank the Goddess.

Chuck raised his glass. "Here's to a successful solstice ritual."

That was something I was more than happy to toast, so I lifted my wine glass as well and clinked it against his. The wine seemed pretty decent, although I had to admit I wasn't an expert or anything. And even better, the warmth of it going down my throat helped to ease some of the tension I'd been carrying in the pit of my stomach ever since I'd agreed to come on this date in the first place.

Maybe Chuck felt it as well. Whatever the reason, the conversation flowed easily enough from there—he talked about the ranch, how his parents had retired and moved to Queen Creek, and he'd taken over running the place. He had one full-time overseer and some seasonal help, but it did sound as if he did most of the work himself. I had to respect that; it wasn't as though he was some sort of soft rich kid who expected everyone else to do the heavy lifting.

Our salads arrived, and were excellent. In between bites, we talked some more, with Chuck describing what it was like to grow up in Globe, and me telling him something of my life in Los Angeles.

"It sounds like another planet," he observed, and inwardly, I had to admit he might be right. L.A. was definitely a law unto itself.

"It's...different," I allowed.

I didn't get any farther than that, however, because in the next moment, I heard a feminine voice that I'd already come to dislike.

"Why, Selena Marx," said Lilith Black. She'd paused a foot or so away from the booth where Chuck and I sat, her two lackeys, as usual, positioned a little ways behind her. "Are you stalking me or something?"

At once, Chuck's brows drew together. From the dismissive way he looked her up and down, it seemed he wasn't terribly impressed. "I doubt it, ma'am," he said in an exaggerated cowboy drawl that made me want to grin, although I managed to maintain my sober expression. "Seeing as how I'm the one who invited Selena here tonight."

Her icy gray eyes glinted with irritation. Obviously, she hadn't missed the look he'd given her... or the way he'd called her "ma'am."

"Oh, well, then," she said, trying to sound casual, even though I could clearly hear the bite in her words. "I suppose it's just the universe putting us on parallel paths."

"What are you doing here at the casino?" I asked. "I thought you were staying in Globe."

"We are," she replied. "I needed a house—the rooms here at the casino wouldn't have suited me at all. But because the elders were so kind about letting me hold my ritual on their land, I thought it would be a good thing to come and have dinner here. I posted about it on Instagram, so I'm sure that'll send more business their way."

Considering how her followers seemed to hang on her every utterance, I had no doubt she was right. As soon as those visitors got to town, they'd probably be heading out to the casino to eat the very same meal that Lilith Black had consumed.

"That was nice of you," I said, figuring I might as well be polite. There was certainly no need to get into a cat fight...even though I could tell she wanted one. Otherwise, she probably wouldn't have seen the need to bring up the tribal elders' largesse again.

"Oh, I do what I can." Lilith paused there, and her Russian Red–lacquered lips pressed together for a moment as she flitted a quick glance toward Chuck. "Enjoy your date. I wouldn't want to keep you from your cowboy."

With that parting shot, she sashayed off, her two assistants in tow. Once again, the Snape lookalike sent me what seemed almost like an apologetic look, although he obviously knew better than to say anything. Some of the other diners stared after them in curiosity, probably because a group who looked like that wasn't exactly a common occurrence in Globe and its environs.

Chuck watched them for a second or two as well before returning his attention to me. "I think that woman has seen *Mean Girls* too many times."

I actually laughed outright—partly because I could never have imagined such a comment coming from Chuck Langdon's lips, and partly because I needed to do something to ease the tension. "Probably," I agreed, then reached for my glass of cabernet and allowed myself a bracing swallow. "I didn't think that was the sort of movie cowboys watched."

He shook his head. "It was a favorite of my ex. Why, I don't know—you'd think she would have recognized more than a little bit of Regina George in herself."

"That bad?"

"Oh, yeah. Except I was too stupid to realize it until we were married." His shoulders lifted, and he picked up his own glass of wine and drank some. "Her walking out was the best thing that ever happened to me."

For a moment, our eyes met, and I stared back at him, not sure what to say. I hadn't really expected him to be quite so brutally honest on a first date. But then, he obviously knew what I'd already begun to realize.

There just weren't a lot of secrets in a place like Globe.

Once again, we were saved by the arrival of the waiter, this time with our entrees. As if both recognizing that it would be better to pay attention to the food for a bit, we dug into our steaks and loaded baked potatoes. And after the moment was safely gone, we discussed logistics about the ritual—where he'd set up barriers to point the crowd in the right direction, whether we should hire someone to direct traffic.

Everything safe and easy.

After dinner, he drove me back to my place. The wine and the good food—and the absence of Lilith Black—should have combined to make me feel mellow. However, tension gripped me as Chuck pulled up next to the spot where my Volkswagen Beetle was parked.

Should I invite him in? No, that would send entirely the wrong message. What if he walked me to the back door and wanted a kiss? The stoop felt awfully exposed, even if no one else actually lived on this block—or the next one. There shouldn't be any witnesses to such an embrace...if it even happened.

He spoke. "I had a really good time."

"So did I," I replied, then added, "Sorry about Lilith."

Chuck only grinned and shook his head. "Nothing you should apologize about. You don't have any control over her actions."

Maybe not, but her presence had still been an unwanted intrusion on our evening. "So…." I said, and paused.

"So." For a long moment, he gazed at me. The only illumination in the vehicle was from the lights on his dashboard and a faint glow from the fixture mounted on the wall next to my building's back door, so it was hard to see much in his expression. If I'd focused, I might have been able to get a glimpse of his aura, but I didn't know if that was such a good idea.

I wasn't sure if I wanted to know what he was thinking.

To my relief, he didn't make a move. He only said, "Let me know about the parking setup. I can see if Travis wants to work it—he could probably use the extra cash."

With those casual words—and the mention of Travis Cox, Globe's one and only Uber driver—I knew Chuck wasn't going to push things, wasn't going to try to lean in for a kiss.

"That sounds like a great idea," I said. "Go ahead and call him."

"Will do."

There didn't seem to be anything left to say, so I said again, "I had a really nice time," then put my fingers on the door handle and let myself out of the truck.

Chuck stayed where he was, watching until I was safely inside and the door locked behind me. I stood there for a moment in the little foyer by the stairs, feeling absurdly relieved.

He might have been the nicest guy in the world…but I knew he wasn't for me.

7

Walmart Revelations

THE NEXT DAY WAS A QUIET ONE. I POSTED several videos on Instagram, along with a photo of my solstice altar setup. Everything seemed to be enthusiastically received—and I'd picked up another ten thousand or so followers—and yet I still had an overwhelming sense of futility.

Or maybe it was just that I hadn't stopped beating myself up about not letting Chuck Langdon kiss me.

It could've been great, I chided myself as I bustled around the kitchen, prepping the ingredients for a big pot of minestrone soup. So what if it was ninety-five degrees outside? One pot of soup —judiciously supplemented with some of my favorite local takeout—would keep me going for a week.

And it was going to be a busy week. This quiet Sunday was just the calm before the storm.

Sure, maybe a kiss from Chuck would have been amazing. Or it could have been a total nightmare. While part of me was still annoyed about the missed opportunity, my deeper self—my gut —told me I'd done exactly the right thing.

And so had Chuck. He hadn't pushed it, had seemed to understand the vibe simply wasn't there.

Under normal circumstances, I would have thought that a man with those kind of instincts was just about perfect. This time, though, I knew that while Chuck Langdon might be perfect for someone, he wasn't perfect for me.

Also, underneath everything else was a silly form of relief. I might have bumped into Lilith Black and her retinue at the Gold Dust Casino's restaurant, but Calvin Standingbear hadn't been anywhere around. Most likely, he hadn't even met the woman.

I had to hope matters would stay that way.

Archie watched my preparations with a sour eye. While every once in a while he would condescend to eat a small piece of chicken or fish, he had absolutely no use for soup.

"I don't see why you feel the need to be so elaborate when you're only cooking for yourself," he groused from a safe vantage point on the dining room rug. I'd grown to love my little flat, but I'd be the first to admit that the kitchen was definitely not built for two...even if the "two" involved were one woman and a cat.

"I like to cook," I said blithely. After more than two months of listening to Archie's complaining, I'd learned to roll with it. I knew that most of the time, he was being a grouch because he didn't have anything better to do. "When you're back in your human form, I'll make you *coq au vin*. You'll love it."

He didn't look terribly thrilled by that offer. "There's the catch—when I'm 'back in my human form.' Which, at the rate you're going, will be never."

"Didn't anyone ever teach you to never say never?" I asked, my tone overly sweet. Yes, Archie still possessed a particular knack for rubbing me the wrong way, but I refused to let him get to me. Lilith Black had already irritated me about as much as I was willing to deal with that week.

"No." Before I could say anything else, he added, "I don't know why you're in such a good mood today. Did the quarterback kiss you good night?"

"No," I replied severely, forgetting the vow I'd taken a while back not to discuss my personal life with my cursed cat. "Nothing happened. And stop calling him 'the quarterback.' His name is Chuck, and he's a nice guy."

"You know what they say about nice guys."

I set down my knife and planted my hands on my hips. It was time to take a break anyway; the onions had started to make my eyes water something fierce. "Don't you have anything better to do?" I asked, blinking the tears away. I knew better than to let my fingers get anywhere near my face.

Archie's broad little nose scrunched. "I'm a man stuck in a cat's body. What do you think?"

Well, he had a point there. Still, I wished he'd leave me to my chopping. I'd been working off some of my antipathy toward Lilith Black by whacking onions, celery, carrots, and mushrooms into neat little chunks, and I didn't feel like having a verbal sparring match with a cat.

I glanced at the clock on the stove. "Well, it's almost two o'clock. Isn't it time for your afternoon nap?"

The look he shot me then was one of sheer annoyance. "I don't nap until two-thirty."

"Sorry—it's hard for me to keep it all straight when you sleep twenty hours out of twenty-four."

My remark seemed to be the final straw for him, because he sent me a malevolent glare before disappearing down the hallway. I'm sure that there were some who would advise me to be patient with Archie, that he'd suffered a great deal and needed to be treated with kindness and forbearance.

Maybe so…but those people had never been forced to live with him.

Cat dispelled for the moment, I returned to my vegetables. Soon enough, they had all been added to the big stockpot I already had simmering gently on a back burner, and I could push one more task over into the "finished" column.

Speaking of which….

Since the soup would keep going the entire afternoon, I left the kitchen and headed into my office. Luckily, Archie was nowhere in sight; he sometimes liked to sleep on the rug in the guest bathroom, and I had a feeling that was where he'd gone.

I'd already made some notes for the ritual, and had decided that although many people celebrated Litha—the pagan midsummer holiday—with ceremonies at noon when the sun would be highest in the sky, I knew that most people attending would much prefer a bonfire…and would also prefer to avoid the searing heat of summer midday in Arizona. Since a fire was also a traditional way of celebrating the solstice, I'd decided on a big bonfire that I'd keep burning until dawn. I'd attended a ceremony like that on the beach, once upon a time. When the sun rose, we'd all made our wishes and affirmations for the coming months, and then jumped over the bonfire's coals to seal our intentions. It had been truly magical, and I wanted to do the same thing this time. Most likely, the vast majority of the attendees would decamp long before dawn, but for anyone with the stamina to last through the night, it should be just as memorable for them as it had been for me that time in Malibu.

Because I'd wanted to avoid any awkwardness between us, I'd already texted Chuck earlier that day to let him know what I was thinking of and if he had any recommendations for places where I could get a good supply of firewood. He'd responded almost immediately, letting me know that he had a huge stockpile at the ranch and that I didn't need to go looking for any wood to buy.

And when I offered to pay him, he refused. Politely, but I could tell he didn't want me to keep shooting down his offers of help. My feelings were so muddled on the topic of Chuck Langdon that I honestly didn't know whether he was still trying to impress me, or whether he just was that nice and I needed to get over myself.

I'd decided to limit the number of tickets to one hundred even. The location I'd be using would probably accommodate more, but that seemed like a decent sized group without getting out of hand. Also, because I planned to make the refreshments myself, I wouldn't get too over-whelmed by trying to feed an army.

No, I wasn't going to go crazy. I'd make honey cakes—a traditional Litha treat—and have platters of fresh fruit, symbolizing summer's bounty. Nonalcoholic punch with fruit, and sparkling water, and also platters of cheese and meat, just because honey cakes, while tasty, didn't have a lot of staying power. It wasn't as though I planned to have a full-on luau with a roast pig or anything like that. But I wanted to provide something for my guests, if only to say thank-you for the way they'd traveled so far afield to attend my solstice ritual.

Even though I hadn't planned for things to be too elaborate, my shopping list was getting longer and longer. And because I knew I had to be at Once in a Blue Moon the next morning to hand out tickets, I realized I needed to do my shopping now.

I gathered up my list, called out, "Archie, I'm going to the store!" and collected my purse from the entry table on the way out the door. No response from the cat…not that I'd really been expecting one. He seemed to view anything I did that wasn't in pursuit of a cure for his curse as a personal affront, and there wasn't much I could do to fix that attitude. I honestly had been researching his problem, but it was slow going, and not exactly the sort of thing I could do twenty-four hours a day, seven days a week.

A blast of hot air met me as soon as I opened the back door to the building. I held back a frown and hoped that the mythical monsoons would be early this year. My duplex back in West Los Angeles had only been about a mile and a half from the beach, and I'd never had to struggle with heat like this before, except on those extremely rare occasions when the wind changed direction and blew hot desert winds across the L.A. basin.

I hoped I'd get used to Arizona summers...eventually.

But because of the little carport/sunshade pavilion Josie's nephew Brett had helped me set up, at least my Beetle had been shielded from the worst of the sun's blast, and the A/C kicked in right away. By the time I got to the Walmart at the western edge of town, I was almost comfortable.

Or rather, I would have been comfortable...if I hadn't spotted Calvin's big white Durango with the tribal police logo on the side, heading right toward me.

My heart began pounding a mile a minute, but I told myself I needed to be cool. After all, we were just passing each other in a parking lot. Perfectly normal.

I caught of glimpse of him inside the SUV,

eyes hidden behind mirrored sunglasses, hair pulled back into its usual ponytail, and I had to grip the steering wheel to force myself to keep going down the aisle I'd chosen. No way of telling whether he'd spotted me or not; my VW Beetle was pretty distinctive, but his gaze had apparently been fixed straight ahead, and that single glimpse wasn't enough to allow me to see whether he'd had any kind of a reaction.

And then the moment was gone. Someone in a shabby old Toyota Camry began to pull out of a space directly ahead of me, and I had to jam on my brakes to avoid crashing into their rear bumper.

Shaking, I took the place the Camry had just occupied and sat behind the wheel for a moment, doing my best to regain my composure. In all the weeks since Calvin had ghosted me, that was the first time I'd actually seen him, unless you could count the one or two times his Durango had gone past on Broad Street just outside my shop.

So what? I asked myself. *It's Sunday, and he needed to go shopping. This wasn't two ships passing in the night. It was just…errands. Get yourself together.*

Good advice. I pulled in a bracing breath, then adjusted my sunglasses and walked as quickly as I could to the front entrance of the store, grabbed a shopping cart, and headed inside.

Since it was a Sunday afternoon, the place was packed. Most of the time, I tried to do my shopping at off hours, a luxury I could afford myself since I had the ability to close up my shop pretty much any time I wanted and take an hour off.

But with the various deadlines for my solstice celebration looming, I didn't have that option today. I had to just suck it up and get the job done.

However, once I started shopping, it didn't seem so bad. I got the feeling that I'd crested a wave of post-church shoppers, and a lot of them were already heading to the checkout stands while I still had plenty of shopping left to do. I gathered up recycled, biodegradable paper plates and cups in the aisle with the picnic supplies, and added a nice selection of cheeses and deli meats to the cart as well. From there, I headed over to the produce section.

To my utter shock, Lilith Black's Snape-looking lackey—assistant...lover...roadie...whatever—was there as well, putting peaches in a plastic bag.

This must have been my day for chance encounters. I knew I should've done a three-card Tarot spread before I'd taken my shower that morning; maybe then I would've had some advance warning of what the universe planned to throw at me that day.

My first instinct was to grab my shopping cart and bolt, but I realized that kind of behavior would only make me more conspicuous.

Besides, he'd obviously spotted me, because he smiled and said, "Hey."

"Hey," I replied cautiously. I hadn't seen any sign of Lilith or her Wednesday Addams surrogate as I wandered Walmart's aisles, but that didn't mean they couldn't be lurking somewhere nearby.

"It's all right," the man said. He sealed off the bag of peaches he was holding with a green twist tie and deposited it in his shopping cart. "Lilith's not here."

"Oh," I said. Was I that transparent?

He wheeled his cart closer to me and extended a hand. "We haven't been formally introduced. I'm Boden Marsh."

"Hi," I responded, then went ahead and shook his hand. He actually had a nice grip, firm without being bone-crushing, and no damp palms, either. And even though I guessed it was redundant because he already knew my name, I went ahead and added, "Selena Marx."

"Stocking up for tomorrow?" he went on, eyeing the contents of my shopping cart.

"Yes," I said. There didn't seem to be much point in denying it. A single woman living alone generally didn't have much use for economy-size blocks of cheese.

"Same here," he said. "Not that we're going to be as elaborate as you. Just some fruit and bread."

I had to wonder why he was being so friendly. Was the niceness a cover to do as much fact-finding about my plans as possible? Maybe, but I somehow doubted it. I had to believe that Lilith was reading my Instagram feed, and so she must know exactly what I was up to.

And actually, I had to admit that up close, Boden wasn't nearly as Snape-like as I'd thought. Dark eyes, yes, but they were a warm, friendly brown, and he had nice laugh lines around them.

"You're probably wondering why Lilith let me off the leash," he added.

Well, I had been, but I wasn't about to admit such a thing out loud. "Um...I'm sure she's getting ready for her ritual, right?" I hedged, figuring that seemed like a safe enough reply.

"That was her excuse," Boden said. "She and Tansy are over at the site. I got sent to run errands because she said she didn't want my masculine vibrations messing up its energy."

Which seemed like an odd sort of thing to say, considering that solstice rituals tended to embrace masculine energy, due to their alignment with the sun. Then again, I didn't know which precise path Lilith Black followed. There were many ways to find one's way to the craft, and I wouldn't presume to guess at the road someone else had taken.

And why was I not surprised that Wednesday Addams' real name was Tansy? It suited her to a, well, T.

"It's probably cooler in here," I observed, and he nodded.

"True. I'm more use running errands anyway. I don't know anything about magic."

Startled, I asked, "You don't?" It seemed kind of odd to me that Lilith had an assistant who couldn't help her in any sort of magical way.

"Nope," Boden replied. "I was drumming in a band when I met Lilith. She said she wanted someone with my kind of energy, and she was offering a lot more than I was getting paid for two or three gigs a month, so here I am."

Now that I'd heard it, Boden's story made a lot of sense. He gave off the vibe of someone who'd been in a band—and I'd met a lot of people like that, thanks to my biological father, Jordan Fairfield. Sure, he was now a respectable music teacher in the Valley, but he still had an air around him that told you he had a wild past. And the same with his friends, almost all of whom had moved on to be insurance agents and contractors and lawyers, but who still didn't feel entirely on the straight and narrow.

I had to wonder if Lilith had chosen Tansy as

her assistant because she also had the right vibe and the right look. It did seem that almost everything for Lilith was based on surface impressions.

Not that I would ask…and I also wouldn't ask Boden if he was "with" Lilith. From the way he'd spoken, I got the feeling that he wasn't, but none of it was any of my business.

Before I could respond to his comment, he went on, "Actually, Lilith doesn't really, either. Know about magic, I mean."

For a second, I could only boggle at him. Somehow, I found my voice and managed to say, "But she's—"

"A famous Instagram witch," he cut in. "I know." A pause as a wry smile touched his thin lips. "Don't you know that being internet famous is mostly smoke and mirrors?"

"Not really," I admitted. "I mean, I just started on Instagram a few days ago."

"And you're the real deal, which is part of the reason why Lilith is gunning for you. She doesn't want you to discover her big secret."

"But you're telling me now," I said, and he shrugged. Even though it was probably pushing a hundred degrees outside, he still wore a long-sleeved black button-up shirt, although the sleeves were rolled up, showing off an impressive array of tats.

"I figured I'd level the playing field," he

replied. If he was at all concerned about Lilith finding out that he'd been blabbing her secrets to me, he didn't show any sign of it. And actually, in a way, I thought I understood. He disliked her business practices, but not enough to make a clean break and lose a steady paycheck. By confiding in me, he could be subversive without risking too much. "You seem like a nice person. I didn't want to see you get flattened by the Lilith Black wrecking ball."

"Um…thanks." I hesitated, then asked, "But why the whole witch thing if she doesn't even believe in it?"

Boden reached up to run a hand through his hair. I couldn't see any obvious roots, which meant even if he darkened it a bit to be pure black, it must still naturally be a fairly dark brown. "She decided it was a good angle for her. A few years ago, she saw people getting famous on YouTube and Instagram, and she wanted a piece of the action. Since she didn't have any real talents, she researched what sort of content would be a good fit for her and decided on witchery. After all, it's not like you can really prove magic is real one way or another, is it?"

Good question. True magic wasn't throwing fireballs or flying on a broomstick or whatever fantasies tended to get perpetuated by the media. It was all about concentrating your energies and setting intentions, and allowing your own energy to merge with that of the universe. Magic definitely worked…I wouldn't have won that first small lottery back in California or found my way to Globe if it didn't…but it wasn't nearly as showy as most people wanted to believe.

"Not really," I said. "You either believe in it, or you don't. And if you can manifest the things you need just by sheer grit, you don't really need magic."

An approving light flickered in Boden's eyes. "Exactly. Lilith's good at grit. And hustling…and leaving a trail of bodies in her wake, if that's what it takes."

I chuckled, although my laugh sounded nervous even to me. "I hope you're speaking metaphorically."

"I am…for now." He paused there, and his expression, which had been mainly amused, sobered immediately. "Lilith really doesn't like competition."

"I'm not competition," I protested. "I'm not trying to get a gazillion followers, or whatever. Honestly, I started this whole thing just as a way to get more tourists to visit Globe. Josie Woodrow put me up to it."

My revelation seemed to relax him a bit. At any rate, that little quirk had returned to his mouth, an indication that he wasn't quite as worried as he'd been a moment earlier. "I believe you. Still, it's better to stay out of Lilith's way."

"I will," I said, which was only the truth. I had absolutely no desire for our paths to cross any more than they already had. "Really, this is just me doing what I can to get Globe on the map."

Boden didn't immediately reply. Maybe he was trying to decide whether I was telling him the simple truth or whether I had some kind of other angle to my Instagram account that I simply didn't want to reveal. When he spoke, however, he only said, "Do what's right for you. Don't let Lilith scare you off. Just...be careful."

"I will," I replied.

That seemed to be enough reassurance for him. He said, "I need to get going, or Lilith's going to wonder what I'm up to. Good luck with your ritual."

Although he didn't add, *You're going to need it,* I got the impression that was exactly what he'd been thinking. He took hold of his shopping cart and began to push it toward the checkout counter, while I watched him go.

So...Lilith Black was a fake. I didn't know why I should be so surprised, except that I knew I would never have the *cojones* to pull that kind of a con with several million people looking on. But, as Boden had pointed out, who would ever be able to tell? From the outside, she was a huge success, had manifested the lifestyle of her dreams and the sort of following most people could only imagine.

And maybe that was its own form of magic, even if it wasn't the kind of magic I practiced.

I let out a sigh and went over to thump a few watermelons. My rival might have been fake, but I wasn't...and I had a lot of work left to do.

8

Change of Heart

I'D WORRIED THAT NO ONE WOULD SHOW UP to claim any tickets to my solstice ritual, and I'd be left with a pile of cheese, sausage, and fruit… not to mention several bags of flour and containers of honey, purchased so I could make my little Litha cakes. But people flowed in and out of the shop all day, buying various odds and ends, picking up their free tickets for the ceremony. Not in huge numbers—I had a feeling we'd probably be a little under capacity—but enough that I guessed my worries had been for naught.

Hazel had already offered to help me out in any way I needed, so I'd asked her to watch the refreshment tables and replenish the platters as necessary. Chuck was already handling the overall logistics of the event, although he'd gotten Travis to do traffic control and keep an eye on the attendees' cars while they were occupied at the ritual site.

And Josie had told me that she'd "drop in," although she couldn't promise she'd be there for the whole thing. "Tuesday night is bridge night, you know," she told me.

Since I'd been subjected to the minutiae of her schedule for the past two months, I'd been able to respond, "Oh, I know. And I know you can't miss it. But the bonfire won't even start up until nine o'clock, since I want to wait until full dark."

Her expression had indicated that she wasn't terribly thrilled by the prospect of tromping around in Chuck's back forty in utter darkness, although I knew it wouldn't be *too* dark. We'd have a waxing gibbous moon that was nearly full, along with a bunch of citronella oil torches to light the way. I wanted to do this ritual correctly, but I also didn't want to get eaten alive by mosquitoes in the process, or have someone break a leg because they tripped over something in the dark.

I hadn't told anyone about my conversation with Boden Marsh, partly because I had the feeling he'd told me those things in confidence, and partly because I didn't know whether anyone would even believe me if I told them that Lilith Black was an utter fraud. It would probably sound like sour grapes on my part, like I didn't want to admit that someone else was a better witch than me.

For all I knew, it was some sort of weird test to see if I could keep a secret. To what purpose, I had no idea, but years of working with clients and doing readings for them had taught me that sometimes people's motivations were beyond screwy. It was a relief to know I didn't have to do that anymore and could focus on the much more straightforward task of keeping my store running. I'd enjoyed doing readings, and yet I was happy to have left that part of my life behind.

And you know? Scratch that. Most of the time, people's motivations were definitely beyond screwy. Ordering inventory was much simpler.

Anyway, by the time the end of Monday afternoon rolled around, I'd given out seventy-two tickets, and there was also part of Tuesday remaining to hand out the rest. I planned to close the shop early on Tuesday afternoon so I could focus on the final bits and pieces of my preparations, but that still gave people a few hours to come by and get a ticket.

And if they didn't, no big deal. I was fine with seventy-five attendees. That was still enough to make the work worthwhile.

Beneath it all was the knowledge I'd held close to the vest, that Tuesday, June twenty-first, was my thirtieth birthday. I didn't know exactly why I felt the need to keep the date a secret, except I really didn't want anyone to make a big deal about it. My life was such that I already had pretty much everything I needed, and I didn't want anyone—specifically, Josie or Hazel—to fuss about buying me presents or trying to take me out to lunch, or whatever. Better to let the day pass while I was in service to the greater powers of the universe.

When I woke up Tuesday morning, though, it was to a stomach knotted tight with nerves. I'd done my best to tell myself that everything was going to be all right, and I honestly had tried to cover as many bases as possible in the limited amount of time I'd had to plan. Even so, that awful sensation of impending doom was back.

I tried to keep those apocalyptic feelings at bay by having a strong cup of coffee to get the day started, and then by making sure I was busy the whole morning. Some more people trickled into the shop to get tickets, rounding up the number to an even ninety.

Just as I was about to take the "be back at" sign and hang it on the door, signaling that the store would be closed until Thursday morning—no way was I going to drag myself into the shop on Wednesday after being up all night the day before—Lilith Black came sailing in, her assistant Tansy trailing a few feet behind her.

No sign of Boden, which was probably a good

thing. I'd never been known for having a good poker face, and I had a feeling I probably would have sent off some sort of subconscious signal to indicate he and I were a bit better acquainted than Lilith believed.

"Hi," I said cautiously, since it wasn't as though I could ignore her outright.

"I just wanted to drop in and wish you the best of luck tonight," Lilith said. That day, she was still wearing black from head to toe, but her dress this time was almost diaphanous, a filmy draped thing that left her arms bare and made her look a little bit like a goth Titania. "But I'm sure you'll do just fine, considering your limited resources."

Oh, how I wanted to throw back in her face that I knew she was a complete fraud, that she didn't know any more about magic than I did about brain surgery. Somehow, though, I held the words in. If nothing else, I didn't want to get Boden in trouble. Oddly enough, I kind of liked the guy. He had a no-nonsense way about him that I appreciated, despite his Snape-masquerading-as-a-goth-dude appearance.

"I hope so," I said mildly.

My gaze shifted past her to Tansy, who had her phone out and appeared to be doing her best to film the exchange while escaping any notice.

"Um…what's she doing?"

Lilith's gray eyes glinted with annoyance, but

she put on a fake-looking smile and said, "Oh, she's just following me around and getting everything on camera. You don't mind, do you?"

Considering I'd gone to work that morning in jeans, a plain blue sleeveless top, and hardly any makeup, I knew I wasn't exactly in the best shape for a close-up. However, letting Lilith see that she'd irritated me didn't seem like a very wise course of action, so I managed to smile as I replied, "Not at all. I can see why you'd want to document your entire trip."

Her smile slipped a little; I could tell she hadn't wanted me to be quite so magnanimous. "Well, thanks. And again, good luck tonight."

She stuck out a hand, and I realized I'd have to shake it or be recorded for all time looking like a petty wench. Gritting my teeth, I extended my hand as well, and shook hers. Unlike Boden's, her grip was the proverbial limp fish, and moist to boot.

But it was over soon enough, although my psychic powers seemed to have deserted me for the moment, since her aura remained hidden and I hadn't gotten a single glimmer of her intentions from that limp handshake. The fake-looking smile returned, and she said, "Have a happy Litha," just before she turned and headed out the door.

Well, at least she knew the traditional name of the holiday. Then again, Boden hadn't said that she didn't do her research, only that she didn't believe in magic and didn't actually practice the craft.

Whatever. It annoyed me that she was so cavalier about something so important, but I knew my disapproval probably meant bupkis to her.

Almost as soon as the door had shut, I hurried over and locked it, and hung up my little "be back at" sign. I glanced down at my hand, still feeling the stickiness of Lilith's touch, but I didn't see any stains or other signs that something had been actually wrong with her.

No, she probably just used goopy hand lotion.

Even so, it felt good to hurry upstairs and take a quick shower, then to spend more time than I normally would on my hair and makeup. Hazel had said she'd try to film as much of the ritual as she could, and I wanted to make sure I looked decent.

Of course, the weather was hot enough that I'd probably sweat off most of that makeup by the time I was done.

I reassured myself that it would be cooler under the trees. Besides, we wouldn't even be starting until after dark.

Starting the ceremony, that is. I needed to be at Chuck's ranch hours before then to get things set up. He'd already offered one of his spare bedrooms for me to change, since wrangling chairs and tables while wearing some kind of Stevie Nicks–inspired getup wasn't a very good idea.

Archie wasn't thrilled to be given his supper early; that cat hated any deviation from his schedule. More than once, I'd wanted to ask him if his birthday had been in late August or September, or maybe in January, but I had a feeling he wouldn't be thrilled with that line of questioning. Still, considering his insistence on a strict routine, I figured he had to be a Virgo, or maybe a Capricorn.

Despite his grousing, I got out the door on time and drove over to Shady Oaks Ranch, the little bag that contained my change of clothes sitting on the front seat of my Beetle, and the trays of food carefully stacked in the back. All during my preparations, I'd wondered just what Lilith had been up to with her little visit to the shop. Doing her best to put me off balance right before the event? Or had she just wanted to catch some unflattering images of me on her assistant's cell phone camera?

Either way, I didn't believe her "best of luck" wishes for a second. If she'd been an actual practicing witch, I might have worried that she would put some kind of a hex on my ritual to make sure it went badly. As it was, she'd probably been positioning herself to look generous and friendly, even though such behavior was a complete lie.

And all right, I couldn't deny that the thought had crossed my mind of putting a little jinx on her own festivities. Nothing that would cause harm to anyone, but something like making sure all the wood she'd ordered for her Litha bonfire would be damp enough that it wouldn't burn properly, would smoke everyone right out of the clearing.

In the end, I'd pushed those negative thoughts aside. I didn't want to stoop to Lilith Black's level. Also, putting bad stuff out in the universe like that invariably had it come shooting right back at you, like a negative-energy boomerang. Better to take the high ground.

Besides, she'd be gone in a few days. And honestly, I'd begun to seriously consider whether I should get rid of my Instagram account once this was all over and done. It seemed to be far more trouble than it was worth. Yes, a bunch of people had been attracted to Globe—and it sounded as though they were shopping and dining and spending money in the area, which was the whole point of this little adventure—but I hadn't signed up to be the town's one-woman Chamber of Commerce. Miriam Jacobsen could handle that sort of thing. It was her job, after all.

Better to be done with the whole affair. If I

deleted my Instagram, I was sure people would forget all about me sooner rather than later. After all, that was sort of the point of social media—people were always chasing the shiny new thing. Soon enough, I wouldn't be even a blip…and I thought I'd be just fine with that.

I pulled up by the main house at Chuck's ranch. Even as I was getting out of the car, he emerged from the front door and came down to meet me.

"Hey," he said as I got out of the car.

"Hey," I responded, glad he was keeping things casual.

"Let's put your stuff in the house," he told me, one hand lifted to shield his eyes from the sun, which had slipped to the west but was still plenty bright. "I've already got tables set out in the clearing, but we should go check to make sure they're where you want them."

Not for the first time, I wanted to kick myself for being so obsessed with Calvin Standingbear—for no good reason, as far as I could tell—that I couldn't even see when something great was right in front of my face. Some psychic I was.

But chemistry wasn't something you could turn on and turn off like a faucet, so I knew there wasn't much I could do to change the situation, no matter how much inner chiding I might inflict on myself. Instead, I sent Chuck a grateful smile and said, "Sounds good."

I slipped my weekender bag over one arm, and then the two of us extracted the trays and food from the back of the car. The cheese and meat were pre-sliced, the Litha honey cakes sitting on their own plates, but I'd left cutting up the fruit for the last minute, since I didn't want anything to get bruised or dried out.

"Right this way," Chuck said.

He led me into the house, which was a big two-story ranch-style home with a little too much knotty pine paneling for my taste. Still, it suited the property, with its big roughly carved beams, leather furniture, and a large stone fireplace that took up most of one wall in the living room.

I didn't have much time for more than that one glance, however, because he headed straight for the kitchen. It was a large, friendly space with green tile counters and a big stainless-steel refrigerator—good thing, because my goodies took up most of the shelf space.

Once all the food was safely stowed away, Chuck took me up to the second floor where the bedrooms were located. Just off the landing was a guest room with a queen bed in an iron bedstead, a plain pine dresser, and not much else.

"You can put your things in here," he said. "And there's a bathroom down the hall."

"Perfect," I replied as I put my little week-ender bag with my change of clothes down on the bed.

"Want any water or anything before we head out to the site?"

I shook my head. "No, I'm good. But thanks."

After that, we went back downstairs and out the back door, Chuck leading me through the pasture and into the wooded area just beyond. The cows were conspicuously absent; obviously, he'd already moved them out of harm's way. A series of wooden stakes with blue fabric fluttering from them marked the path from the open spot by the garage where the cars would park through the pasture and on into the woods, guiding us all the way to the clearing.

He'd actually done much more than merely set up tables. Yes, they were there, placed off to one side, but in addition, he'd already put out the wood for the bonfire, and made a neat stack of extra logs not too far away so it would be easy to add them as needed. The tables were covered in dark blue cloths, and there were also several rows of chairs set out in addition to the tables.

I looked at the setup, more and more impressed. Chuck must have picked up on my vibe, because he said, "I figured people might want a chance to sit down at some point. There's not enough for everyone, but I thought it would help."

"It's great," I told him. "I should have thought of that myself. But where did you get all this stuff?"

I really hoped he hadn't gone out and spent money on supplies from an event company or something. To my relief, his next words disabused me of that notion.

"Oh, my parents had a big fortieth anniversary party here before they moved to Queen Creek. I've had all this stuff stored out in the garage ever since then. It's kind of nice to be able to use it for something."

"Well, thanks," I said, knowing even as I spoke that the words were totally inadequate. "This is really going above and beyond."

He grinned then, blue eyes crinkling with what appeared to be hidden laughter. "Well, I wanted to help you show up that Lilith Black chick. She's really a piece of work."

Since I couldn't exactly argue with that statement, I just nodded and gave him a smile of my own. "I don't even know what she has planned. Honestly, it doesn't matter. This isn't a contest. Besides, I gave away almost all of my tickets, so it's not like people are abandoning my celebration in droves so they can go to hers."

Chuck nodded, relief clear in his expression.

"That's good to hear. But if everything here looks good to you, we might as well head back to the house."

Since I couldn't really improve on the setup, I agreed that we were done in the clearing until it was time to bring out the food. Despite being shielded by the trees, the sun beating down from the west was still pretty fierce, and I was fine with staying inside until it had disappeared behind the horizon. That wouldn't be for a few more hours, but I needed to get the food trays set up.

Just as we were approaching the house, Hazel pulled up in her dusty old Volvo. She emerged from the station wagon, looking très Globe chic in a sleeveless embroidered blouse, skinny jeans, and tan cowboy boots. The afternoon light caught in her medium brown hair, turning the paler streaks almost gold.

"Who's that?" Chuck asked, staring at her as if mesmerized.

"My friend Hazel Marr," I replied, even as I tried not to smile. I'd seen that look on men's faces enough times to know what the glazed expression in his eyes probably meant. "She's an artist in town. I thought you two knew each other."

"Well...." The word trailed off, and he ran a distracted hand through his hair. "I guess I maybe met her in passing, but I never...."

Once again, his words disappeared into the

ether, and he suddenly looked embarrassed, as if he'd just realized he was goggling at another woman while he stood next to the one he'd taken out to dinner just the night before.

If I'd had any designs on him, I might have been offended. As it was, I could only be glad that, for whatever reason, his eyes had suddenly been opened. Maybe that little half-intention I'd sent out on Hazel's behalf a few days earlier was starting to work...only in a way I hadn't imagined.

Apparently oblivious to our exchange, Hazel approached, one hand lifted in greeting. "Hi. I'm ready to be put to work."

"Great," I said, glad of the chance to jump in and get things moving. Chuck's expression suddenly turned brisk, and I guessed he'd also realized that it was probably better to focus his attention on everything that needed to get done in the next couple of hours. "We've still got a lot of prep to do in the kitchen."

The three of us headed inside, and Hazel and I got to work cutting up the mounds of fruit I'd bought and arranging it on a variety of platters and trays. Chuck disappeared, ostensibly to set out all the citronella torches, but I think he was mostly glad to have a reason to remove himself from our company. I'd caught the couple of side-long glances he'd sent Hazel's way, and I knew he was trying to be sure he didn't make a fool of himself.

Of course, I knew any advances he made would probably meet with a friendly reception. Or at least, they would once she knew there was absolutely nothing going on between him and me.

"You two seem to be getting along really well," she remarked as she expertly cut a papaya into neat slices.

"Oh, Chuck and me?" I said in an off-hand tone. "He's a nice guy. I think we've both figured out we do better as friends than as anything more, though."

Her hands went still then, knife resting on the cutting board. "You're not backing off because of what I told you the other day, are you?"

"No," I said hastily. "There's just no spark, you know? He's a great guy, but…."

I let the words trail off, figuring I'd said enough. Speculation flickered in Hazel's greenish eyes, but I got the feeling she wouldn't probe further. Also, I caught pale blue flickers in her aura before they disappeared, telling me she was relieved…even if she wasn't about to say anything out loud. No doubt she was thinking that even if she didn't have a future with Chuck, she at least wouldn't have to deal with the awkwardness of her friend dating a guy she was attracted to.

Time to stay silent, though. I had no doubt

the universe would show its intentions regarding their relationship soon enough.

In the meantime, there were trays to carry out to the clearing and the rest of the setup to be completed. Once all that had been done, I disappeared into the guest bedroom to change into my outfit for the ritual—a pretty green gown I'd ordered from Holy Clothing while I was still back in L.A., vaguely medieval in style, with a low scoop neck and the sacred triple moon embroidered on the front.

Might as well look like a witch, after all.

I hung a pentagram set with moonstones around my neck, and put silver drops in my ears and a variety of silver rings on my fingers. No bracelets, because I always felt as though they got in the way when I was performing a ritual.

Chuck and Hazel were in the living room, waiting for me. As I walked in, her eyes widened slightly.

"Wow, Selena—you really look the part."

"That's the point, I suppose." With both of them staring at me, I couldn't help feeling a little self-conscious. Tone light, I added, "After all, I have to be Instagram-ready, right?"

Hazel chuckled, and Chuck gave a very small shake of his head. "Speaking of which," she said, "do you want me to film the festivities with my phone, or with yours?"

"You can use mine," I said. In fact, I'd brought it downstairs with me for that very reason, and I handed it over to her. "The code is 8311."

The two of them looked a little surprised that I'd just blurt out the access code to my phone like that, but honestly, I wasn't worried about it. I knew I could trust them. Besides, I wasn't one of those people who kept their entire life on their phone. I knew there wasn't anything on my iPhone that was at all embarrassing, except maybe some old texts from my mother asking me whether I was dating anyone.

Unfortunately, the answer to that question had stayed the same for quite some time.

By that point, it was a little past seven-thirty. On the tickets I'd had Dave print up for me, I'd stated that the gates to the property would be opening at eight, but I had a feeling there would be a couple of early birds.

There always were.

I put on a smile, trying to ignore the nervous butterflies in my stomach. "Okay," I said. "I think it's showtime."

9

Solstice

SOMEWHERE INSIDE, I'D HARBORED THE FEAR that people still wouldn't show up, despite how many tickets I'd given out. It seemed like just the sort of trick Lilith Black would play on me—to have her followers dutifully troop over to the store to get their admission to my solstice ritual, only to make sure they'd all be over at her own ceremony, leaving me with a pile of uneaten food on the tables Chuck had set out…and a whole mess of egg on my face.

And unfortunately, my gut seemed to have been correct. Travis was ready and waiting to park cars, but the only one that appeared was Josie's red Cadillac sedan, which bumped its way across the pasture and seemed vaguely annoyed by being subjected to such an indignity.

She got out, gingerly making her way along the path that Chuck had marked out with care, using surveyor's sticks and citronella torches. I saw all this because I was standing at the edge of the grove, vainly hoping that someone…anyone… would show up.

"But where are all your guests?" she asked, looking around in bewilderment.

"Best guess, they're over at Lilith Black's ritual," I replied. Bitterness seeped into my tone despite my best efforts to keep it out.

Her pale blue eyes—looking somehow even paler in the flickering light from the torches— widened slightly. "How rude!"

My thoughts exactly. However, I didn't much see the point in going on a tirade as to why Ms. Black was a conniving wench. I'd been outplayed, and there didn't seem to be much I could do about it.

"I suppose," I said. "But come on—we have a lovely bonfire going, and there's lots of food."

Lots and *lots* of food. I didn't really care about the money I'd wasted purchasing all those supplies, but I really hated the idea of all that lovely fruit going to waste. Maybe there was someplace we could donate it before it went bad.

Josie's lips tightened, but she took another look at my face and apparently decided that she'd better not push things. In uncharacteristic silence, she followed me into the clearing, where Chuck and Hazel were standing and doing their best to make conversation.

And my comment about the bonfire had been true enough. The wood Chuck had provided was well seasoned, and had blazed up without any encouragement from nasty chemical starters. With the sun down, the air had cooled, and it was pleasant enough out there under the trees. I'd worried that the fire would make things too hot, but I'd forgotten how much of a difference some altitude could make when it came to dropping nighttime temperatures.

Everyone was staring at me, and I pulled in a breath. What the heck was I supposed to say?

Well, practical matters first, I suppose.

"I know this isn't what any of us planned on," I said, trying to ignore Hazel's sympathetic expression, Josie's look of righteous indignation…the hard, angry set to Chuck's mouth. My friends, and despite my anger toward Lilith Black, I couldn't help but feel a rush of affection for all of them. I was still a newcomer here, but they clearly looked at me as one of their own. "It's still the solstice, however, and I still have a ritual to perform. Before I get started, though—Josie, is there something we can do with all this food?"

She glanced over at the tables Chuck had so thoughtfully set up. "I think the shelter down on Third Street would love to have it. Let me make a quick call."

I sent her a grateful look, and she pulled her phone out of her purse. Even though it was nearly nine o'clock at night, whoever she was calling must have picked up right away, because she said, "Hello, Eva? It's Josie. Would you be able to take some trays of fresh fruit tonight? I can bring them over in…." She trailed off there and sent me a questioning look.

"I should be done around nine-thirty," I said, and she nodded.

"About an hour," she finished. "Is that all right?" A pause as she waited for the reply. Then she said, "Thank you, Eva—you're a godsend."

And after that, Josie slipped her phone back in her purse.

"All settled. Eva runs the women's shelter, and she's there all the time, so that's why I thought she would be the best person to call. And yes, she'll take everything."

"Thanks so much, Josie," I said, hoping she could hear the gratitude ringing through my words.

She waved her hand. "It's no bother. I'm glad we could have something good come of all this."

Something good. That was what I needed to

hold in my heart, the reason why I was here. So what if Lilith Black had pulled a dirty trick on me? True, I didn't have any concrete evidence of foul play, but my instincts told me she was most likely behind all the no-shows. Anyway, this ritual was about gratitude, about acknowledging the power of the change of seasons and the gifts it brought to our lives. One petty woman couldn't change any of that.

"Then I'll go ahead and get started," I said. "That way, you won't be too late getting over to the women's shelter."

"I can help with that, too," Hazel put in. "There's lots of room in the back of my Volvo."

"And I'll also lend a hand if you need it," Chuck added.

Josie clasped her hands together. "Oh, that would be wonderful. Yes, we can make short work of all this—although it's probably better if you stay in the car while we're bringing the food into the shelter, Chuck. Those women have been through so much."

For a second he looked puzzled, as if he couldn't quite comprehend what she was talking about. But then he nodded, apparently realizing that the presence of a man at a women's shelter might be triggering for the people who'd taken refuge there. "No problem."

Seeming to understand that was settled, Josie

looked back over at me. "What do you need us to do?"

"Well, you can stand or sit," I told her. "Whatever's most comfortable for you."

"I think she should stand," Hazel said. "The light here is uncertain enough that I think if Josie and Chuck stand over there"—she waved with the hand that wasn't holding my phone—"then I can film the fire so it looks as if there are more than two people watching."

While I appreciated the offer, I didn't think there was much point in trying to fool anyone on Instagram. Actually, there wasn't any point in filming the ritual at all.

"Don't worry about it," I replied. "There's no need to get this down for posterity. In fact, I'm going to delete Instagram off my phone as soon as this night is over."

Josie opened her mouth as if to protest, then shut it again. I had no idea what I looked like right then, but whatever she saw in my face, she realized there wasn't much point in arguing with me.

"If that's what you want," she said, sounding uncharacteristically defeated.

"It is," I said firmly. "So you all can sit or stand or do whatever feels most comfortable for you. This won't take very long."

Earlier in the day, I'd made up a pouch filled

with lavender and chamomile, and tied it with a red string, and hidden my petition for peace and prosperity…and yes, love…within. I'd told Hazel she could do the same thing, but she'd only given me a small smile and said she had just about everything she wanted already.

Maybe that was true…or maybe she just hadn't been quite ready to put her trust in a faith that must have felt very foreign to her.

Anyway, my pouch was the only one I dropped into the fire as I spoke the words of the ritual.

"Great God, Father of the Earth,
    Shine down on this, your strongest day.
    Blessed Goddess who gave us Birth,
    Bless us who honor your ancient way.
    As Summer's light falls to the ground,
    lending crops and trees its power,
    the Summer winds blow warm and round,
    touching the corn silk and the flowers.
    We give you thanks, our Mother Earth,
    We praise you, fire of the Sun.
    We dance this Solstice eve with Mirth,
    from evening's last light 'til the night is done."

. . .

Then it was time to walk around the bonfire holding the snuffer I'd brought with me, to put out the candles at the four quarters of the circle I'd drawn after the bonfire was first lit. One by one, I snuffed the candles, thanking them for their service and for the energy they'd brought to my observance. When I was done, I turned to see all three of my friends watching me with wide eyes.

"Why, that was beautiful!" Josie exclaimed, looking somehow surprised.

"What, did you think I was going to sacrifice a goat or something?" I responded wryly.

One hand flapped in a flustered gesture. "Well, no, of course not, but…." She stopped there, as if she'd realized that anything she said would only make matters worse. "I supposed it just wasn't what I was expecting."

"A lot of witchcraft is simply acknowledging the power of the earth…the sun and the moon and the stars," I said. "It's a very natural obser-vance. That's why we perform these rituals at times of power like the solstice and the equinox. There's nothing terribly mysterious about them."

As Josie nodded, Hazel stepped up and gave my arm a sympathetic squeeze. "It really was love-ly," she said. "And the loss of all those jerks who took tickets and couldn't be bothered to show up."

I knew she'd said that only to comfort me, but her words were truer than she knew. The people who'd gone to attend Lilith Black's ritual might have gotten more of a show, but there wouldn't be any real power behind it. She didn't know what she was doing, couldn't invoke the power of the four quarters and the hidden sun at its strongest. If they'd come here and cast their own petitions into the fire, they might have been able to accomplish something meaningful. As it was, they'd go home and have nothing to show for their trip.

But at least they'd come here. In that way, Josie's wish had been fulfilled, because those tourist dollars had flowed into Globe, even if they hadn't necessarily come my way.

"Well," she said, suddenly brisk. "I suppose we might as well get all this food over to the shelter— if you're done here, Selena."

I was. Or at least, I'd finished this part of the ceremony. I still planned to hold my vigil here all night, even if that vigil would turn out to be a solitary one. Tucked away into a pocket of my skirt was another petition, a very private one. I would throw it onto the fire when I was alone.

However, I didn't say anything about that. No, I only helped Josie and Hazel and Chuck carry the trays of fruit and Litha cakes to Josie's and Hazel's cars. Once that was done, I said, "I'm going to stay here, if it's okay."

Chuck raised an eyebrow. "I know earlier you

said you were going to keep a vigil by the bonfire all night, but...."

But that had been back when I thought I'd be surrounded by dozens of solstice observers. I had to admit that the thought of staying in the clearing all night felt a bit scary. After all, only a few months earlier, Calvin Standingbear had warned me that the areas around town were populated by snakes and coyotes and bobcats and maybe even bears.

Of course, he'd been talking about the land down by the San Ramon River on the reservation, and not Chuck Langdon's ranch. It had to be a bit safer here, didn't it? The entire property was surrounded by a combination of barbed-wire and split-rail fences, although I had a feeling all that fence had been constructed to keep the cows in and not necessarily to keep wildlife out.

"It should be safe enough, shouldn't it?" I asked.

His shoulders lifted ever so slightly. "I suppose so. I mean, I can't guarantee that there won't be some coyotes wandering around the perimeter of the property, but they should stay well clear of the fire. As long as you keep it going, you should be all right." A pause, and then he added, "I can loan you one of my rifles, just in case."

Giving me a gun would probably be more hazardous than leaving me to brave a pack of coyotes on my own. "I don't know how to shoot," I said. "City girl, remember?"

That comment earned me a grin. "It was just a thought."

"I can come back and stay with you," Hazel offered, but I shook my head.

"No, I don't expect you to do that. I'll be fine."

She looked troubled—and Josie didn't seem too thrilled by my decision to camp out in the clearing all night, either—but they didn't offer any further protests, only headed off to their cars so they could get the food safely to the Third Street Shelter. I was happy to see Chuck climb into the passenger seat of Hazel's Volvo, and hoped that, even though this evening had turned out to be a complete bust for me, maybe at least those two would get the happy ending they deserved.

Despite the crackling of the fire, the clearing felt preternaturally quiet when I returned alone. We'd left out the pitchers of water and cups on the beverage table, so I went ahead and poured myself some and then took a seat in one of the empty chairs.

Was I crazy for doing this? It wasn't as though I was a squire, performing a vigil so I could be knighted the next day and given my sword and shield. At the same time, though, I thought it might be necessary, if only to quiet my mind and reflect on what was truly important.

Lilith Black might have tried to hurt me, but she'd only succeeding in showing me that I had some true friends in Globe. That was more than worth all the trouble she'd put me through.

From somewhere off in the distance came the hollow, haunting cry of an owl. I couldn't see the bird, but I imagined it in my mind's eye anyway, the wide, pale wings, the round golden eyes. Had it caught its prey, or would it keep hunting through the night?

Oddly, the realization that an owl was out there somewhere in the dark made me feel a little less lonely. And really, I knew I wasn't all that alone; sooner or later, Chuck would come home and go to sleep in the big ranch house. Maybe he would dream of Hazel.

That notion made me think of my own dream. I reached into my skirt pocket and pulled out the little scrap of paper I'd placed there earlier. Just five words, written in black ink on the brown parchment I used specifically for petitions and spells.

I want someone to love.

Maybe that person wasn't Calvin Standing-bear. I had to accept that reality. But I also had to accept that, even though I tried to act as if I didn't care whether or not I had someone to share my world, I didn't want to go through this life alone.

My eyelids drooped, and I blinked. It had been a long, long day. Would I be able to stay awake all night so I could place my petition in the smoldering coals of the bonfire?

At the rate I was going, probably not.

Honestly, I should probably just get up from this chair, walk over to my car, and drive home so I could sleep in a proper bed. No one would judge me for bailing out.

But I'd judge myself.

Even so, I thought it was probably a good idea to put the petition in the fire now. It would still have its own power, one guided by the strength of this midsummer night.

I got up from the chair and dropped the little piece of paper into the bonfire. At once, the flames caught hold of the parchment, burning it into ashes even as I watched.

I chose to take that as a good sign.

The task done, I returned to my chair. It was hard and uncomfortable, one of those plastic and metal folding jobs, but it was still probably better than trying to lie on the dead leaves underfoot. A light breeze touched my cheek, and I drank some more water. Right then, I felt as though I'd been caught in an odd, liminal state, sleepy and yet oddly alert, my senses catching everything—the rustle of the leaves overhead, the hot, acrid scent of the bonfire, the cool night wind against my skin, even the faint glow of the waxing moon as it slipped behind the hills to the west.

I was safe here. This place, this little hollow, would protect me.

With that thought in my mind, I slid into sleep…

…only to feel someone's hand on my shoulder, shaking me awake. "Selena!"

Chuck's voice, sounding urgent, worried. My eyes flared open, and I realized that the sun was already slanting through the trees, edging the green canopy overhead with gold.

In the next second, I also sensed that my neck was aching fiercely, thanks to falling asleep in that chair with my head tilted to one side. The discomfort fled, however, as I realized Chuck wasn't alone. Chief Lewis stood a few feet away, and beyond him, expression grimmer than I'd ever seen it, was Calvin Standingbear.

"What's going on?" I asked. My head throbbed, almost as if I'd spent all night drinking, even though no alcohol had passed my lips since my dinner with Chuck two nights earlier.

Calvin and Chief Lewis exchanged a glance, and the Globe police chief's lips compressed. When he opened his mouth, a chill flooded through my body, even though it was already almost too warm outside.

"Lilith Black was found dead this morning," he said, and again he paused.

It was Calvin who spoke next. "I'm going to need to talk to you…now."

10

Usual Suspect

"WE'VE GOT TO STOP MEETING LIKE THIS," I quipped feebly, but Calvin's stony expression didn't change.

So much for trying to lighten the mood. Not that my mood was feeling exactly light right then —it was just that it seemed as if I needed to say something to make this moment seem a little less fraught.

"I'll need you to tell me exactly where you were and what you did last night."

We sat in his office at the San Ramon tribal police station. In a disturbing echo of Lucien Dumond's murder, Lilith's body had also been found by the river, and so the crime was under tribal jurisdiction. Calvin had brought Chief Lewis along with him when he came to find me at Shady Oaks Ranch as a courtesy, nothing more.

And while I'd idly daydreamed about all the ways my path might cross Calvin's one day—our brush-by in the Walmart notwithstanding—I honestly hadn't thought it would be because I'd been hauled in for questioning about yet another murder.

I tilted my head at him and said, "You don't really think I killed Lilith Black, do you?"

Calvin settled against the worn leather seat back of his office chair, dark eyes opaque. As usual, his long black hair was pulled back in a severe ponytail, revealing all the sculpted lines of his high cheekbones and firm jaw. It was actually more difficult to face him than I'd thought it would be, because underneath my worry about the current situation thrummed the constant question of *why.*

Why did you ghost me?

Why did you kiss me in the first place if you were just going to pull a disappearing act?

The door to his office was shut, affording us some privacy. I suppose I could have asked him those questions, since no one would have been able to hear what I was saying.

But the coward in me kept quiet.

"I'm not a judge or jury," he said. "It's not my place to assign guilt or hand out punishment. All I can do is assemble the facts of the case and then pass them on to the D.A.'s office."

He sounded deadly serious, and there wasn't even a hint of warmth in his dark eyes. A chill crept down my spine, and my stomach, already sour thanks to the stale coffee he'd poured for me as a courtesy once we reached the station, performed an uneasy flip-flop.

Did he actually think I was capable of killing Lilith Black?

I swallowed. "I had a solstice bonfire at Chuck Langdon's ranch. It was poorly attended, and so, once I was done with the ceremony, I helped Josie and Hazel load the leftover food into their cars so they could take it over to the Third Street Shelter. I stayed awake a while longer, but I fell asleep not too long after they left."

Calvin made a notation on the yellow pad that lay on the desk in front of him. "What time was that?"

Good question. I hadn't been wearing a watch, and my phone had been tucked away in my dress pocket. And I, still an L.A. girl to the bone, had no idea how to tell the time by the position of the moon or the stars overhead. "I don't know," I said, knowing how weak that response must have sounded. Trying to help, I added, "Maybe around eleven?"

He wrote that down. "And you slept out there in the clearing all night?"

"Yes," I replied, and gave him a rueful smile. "And I have the crick in my neck to prove it."

Not even the faintest twitch of his lips in response to my comment.

Then again, I probably shouldn't have been looking at his mouth.

"Chuck told me he got back to the ranch and went out to check on you a little before midnight. He said you were dead asleep, so he decided not to wake you…he knew you were doing some kind of vigil or something."

Well, it wasn't exactly a vigil, more a way to make my petition more powerful. But I wasn't about to try explaining that to Calvin Standing-bear. "See?" I said. "Chuck saw me at the clearing. I wasn't anywhere near Lilith Black."

"The M.E.'s initial estimate is that she died sometime after midnight, probably around three or four in the morning," Calvin replied. "Which means there was plenty of time for you to leave the property after Chuck came by to check on you."

I crossed my arms and sent him a narrow-eyed glare. "Yes, and my car was parked right next to the house. Don't you think Chuck would've heard me coming and going?"

"Possibly," Calvin allowed. "Or maybe he's a heavy sleeper."

While I supposed that was a possibility, I kind

of doubted it. Because Chuck basically managed the ranch by himself, I had a feeling that he didn't allow himself to slumber too deeply, just in case he had to get out of bed in the middle of the night to look after a sick calf, or take care of whatever other emergencies might pop up at odd hours.

"Maybe you should ask him," I suggested.

Calvin made another note on his pad. "Maybe I will."

This was ridiculous. We might have been strangers. Obviously, he'd gotten cold feet when it came to having any kind of a relationship with me, but had he forgotten that only two months earlier, he'd admitted he didn't think I was capable of murder?

"I didn't kill Lilith Black," I said flatly. "I honestly don't see why you would even think I was a suspect."

He set down his pen and folded his hands on the desktop. I tried not to look at them, because more than once I'd imagined what it would be like to have those long, strong fingers cupping my face, or caressing my hair, or...

...well, or doing all sorts of other things to me, none of which seemed remotely a possibility at the moment.

"Chuck told me about that mean trick she pulled on you," he said. "Apparently, she posted something on Instagram to the effect that her bonfire was the only one worth attending and that you didn't know what you were doing and there was no point attending your ritual. Some people might find that kind of slander sufficient motive."

So that was what had happened. I released a gust of a laugh, derisive and hard. "Oh, please. That was middle school garbage. You think I'm going to let something like that get under my skin? Anyway," I went on before he could respond, "if I were *really* out for revenge, I would have put a hex on her—made all her hair fall out, or have YouTube de-monetize her channel, or whatever. I certainly wouldn't *kill* her."

For just a second, Calvin appeared almost amused. "You can really do something like that?"

"Oh, yes. But," I added, "I choose not to use that kind of magic because it almost always rebounds on the user. It's really not safe."

"I'll take it under advisement."

The great stone face was back. How could I possibly get through to him? It seemed he was willing to believe the worst, no matter what I said. I didn't know what could have caused such a change in his attitude toward me. Was it that in this case, the victim was female, and a rival of sorts?

I supposed such a thing was possible, although

I didn't want to acknowledge that he could believe the worst of me. "How was Lilith murdered?"

He didn't blink. "You know I can't tell you that."

My jaw clenched, but I made myself say calmly enough, "You might as well. I doubt you have enough evidence to hold me, and you also know I have plenty of money to post bail."

"You're not under arrest, Selena."

Oh, right. Calvin had driven me to the station, but so far, I hadn't been formally charged with anything. This little interview was a fact-finding mission and nothing more.

"Still. Anyway, you know that as soon as I'm back in Globe, someone—probably Josie—is going to fill me in on all the gory details. So you might as well spill."

A pained expression had flitted across his face at the word "gory," but he only said, "She was stabbed in the back with her ceremonial dagger."

"An athame," I corrected him automatically, even as I tried not to wince. As a rule, athames weren't very sharp. Someone would have had to drive it into Lilith's back with a great deal of force.

Despite the gruesome mental image Calvin's description had conjured, I couldn't help thinking that the manner of her death sounded like a shining example of instant karma. What better end for a back-stabbing fake witch?

"Right," he said, although his expression didn't shift. Was he thinking of the time he'd gone with me to my apartment to retrieve my own athame so he could have it tested for traces of Lucien Dumond's blood? Of course, those forensic tests hadn't found anything, because in that case—just as in this one—I was totally innocent.

This time, though, Lilith had been stabbed with her own dagger, and so there wouldn't be any evidence on my athame. "Fingerprints?" I asked, knowing I sounded a little desperate.

"No. It was either wiped clean, or the person using it was wearing gloves."

Which told me the murder had probably been a calculated one. You don't pause to put on gloves if you're killing someone in the heat of the moment. I supposed if it had been a crime of passion, the murderer might have stopped afterward to wipe down the knife, but if it had been sticking out of her back, doing so would have presented its own problems.

Before I could say anything, Calvin pulled out a new-looking black iPhone encased in a baggie from a big manila envelope sitting on his desk. "I'd also like you to tell me about this."

"About what?" I asked. "That's not my phone."

"No, it belongs to Tansy McCall, Lilith's assistant." He removed the phone from the baggie, entered a code, and then turned it toward me.

I blinked at the screen, realizing that I was looking at the footage she'd taken the day before, when she'd accompanied Lilith on her little visit to my shop. The expression on my face as I confronted the Instagram witch made it look as though I'd just drunk curdled milk.

Well, I already knew I would've made a horrible poker player.

"It looks like you weren't a very big fan of Lilith Black," Calvin said, his tone now almost dry.

"No, I wasn't," I replied. "But disliking someone intensely isn't a great motive for murder. Otherwise, you police would have a lot more killings to investigate, wouldn't you?"

"Maybe," he allowed.

"I didn't like her coming into my store when I knew her only reason for doing so was to stir the pot," I continued. "Especially since by then I also knew she was a huge fake."

That comment seemed to get to Calvin; he straightened in his chair even as he stopped the video and set the phone back down. "Excuse me?"

"She was a fake," I repeated. "She didn't know anything about real magic or the craft. It was all a show she put on to get followers on Instagram and YouTube."

"And you know this how?" Calvin asked. "Do real witches have a way of sniffing out fakes or something?"

Should I be flattered by the off-hand way he'd called me a "real witch"?

Probably not.

"No," I said. "Her assistant Boden told me."

One of Calvin's eyebrows lifted ever so slightly. "Why would he do that?"

About all I could do was shrug. "I don't know. I think he likes me…or at least, he likes me more than he liked Lilith." I knotted my fingers in my lap and added, "Maybe he's the one you should be talking to. Or Tansy."

"I have spoken with both of them. They both have iron-clad alibis."

Well, crud. Whereas I'd been out in the forest, communing with nature. Maybe I could track down that owl I'd heard the evening before, have him come in and give a deposition that he'd seen me sleeping in the clearing all night.

And actually, I'd thrown out that comment about Lilith's assistants because it seemed much more logical to me that someone close to Lilith had to be the murderer. I actually kind of liked Boden, too, but that didn't mean I thought he was innocent.

Except he apparently had an alibi…as did Tansy.

"Well, it wasn't me," I said briskly. "Maybe you should be questioning the people who attended her ritual last night. The murderer could be some kook who thought they'd gain extra power by killing a witch on Midsummer Eve."

Calvin looked a little taken aback by my suggestion. "Is that actually a thing?"

"No," I said. "At least, not among any of the witches and warlocks I've known. Even Lucien Dumond wasn't the type to be into human sacrifice. All I'm saying is that it isn't outside the bounds of possibility."

He was silent for a moment. "We are questioning the attendees," he told me. "But there were nearly two hundred of them, so that's going to take time. It made more sense to talk to you, since you had a more obvious motive."

Two hundred people. Well, now I knew for sure where the people who'd picked up the tickets for my little ritual had gone...not that I hadn't already suspected it.

Calvin looked tired. Not so surprising; he'd probably been up since dawn...or even before that, but still, a rush of pity went through me. I wished things were different between us, because I would have reached out and taken him in my arms, held him close so I could give him some reassurance that he'd get this figured out.

Obviously, I wasn't in any position to do such a thing.

I cleared my throat. "Is there anything else?"

"No," he said, and I could almost see his jaw harden, as if he realized he'd revealed too much in even those few seconds of vulnerability. "Standard warning—don't leave town without letting me know."

"I don't have plans to go anywhere," I replied. "Well, except back out to Chuck's ranch so I can get my car, but—"

"I'll drive you," Calvin cut in. "Let's go."

He rose from his chair, and I stood as well, taking note of every miscellaneous ache and pain that had resulted from my night out in the open. Good thing I'd already planned to take the day off —I was going to need some time to recover from that little escapade.

As Calvin walked me to his SUV, the summer heat already beating down from above and baking up from the parking lot's asphalt, I belatedly recalled that yesterday had been my birthday.

Heck of a way to turn thirty.

I obviously didn't mention that little fact to Calvin. No, I just buckled my seatbelt and stared straight ahead as he pulled out of the space near the station's entrance that had been reserved for the police chief, and maintained that stony silence all the way back to Chuck's ranch.

As he slowed down to take the turn onto the dirt lane that led to the house, Calvin said, "I am sorry about this, Selena. But I wouldn't be doing my job if I didn't question the most obvious suspect."

"Understood," I replied. And honestly, I did understand. He had to be thorough.

Like him, though, I was just dead tired. I only wanted to go back to my apartment and sleep through the whole day.

Maybe it was exhaustion that finally loosened my tongue.

"Are we going to keep dancing around each other like this?"

His fingers tightened on the steering wheel. "Like what?"

"This. You made me think something was happening between us…and then you pulled a disappearing act. What's going on?"

He didn't look at me. "I realized it wouldn't work out."

"Why not?"

"Lots of reasons."

One of which, I assumed, was that I wasn't a member of the San Ramon Apache tribe. Fair enough. Still, it would have been helpful for him to take that minor detail into account before he led me to believe there might be a future for the two of us.

However, I was too tired then to start an argument. I just sat quietly until he pulled up next to my dusty blue Beetle and came to a stop. Almost at once, the door to the house opened and Chuck emerged, clearly intending to come over and make sure I was okay.

While I knew I should have been glad for his concern, right then I didn't have the energy to care.

Just as I put my hand on the door, I turned toward Calvin and said distinctly, "Too bad you couldn't have figured all that out before you kissed me."

I didn't wait for him to respond, but pushed down on the handle and slid out of the passenger seat. Out of the corner of my eye, I could see the way he stiffened. He didn't make any attempt to stop me, though, only waited stolidly behind the wheel as I slammed the door shut.

Chuck was approaching, but Calvin clearly didn't want to hang around and exchange pleasantries. No, he put his foot on the gas and was off in a cloud of dust before Chuck could reach my car.

He stared after the disappearing tribal police SUV and said, looking puzzled, "He's in a hurry."

"Police business," I remarked, trying not to cough from the dust Calvin's passage had stirred up.

Chuck's eyebrows were quizzical, but he only said, "Are you okay?"

"I'm fine," I replied. "He wanted to hear my story, but there's no real evidence connecting me to Lilith's murder except the fact that I had a beef with her. That's not the sort of thing that'll hold up in court, though."

"So…you're not under arrest?"

Not yet, I thought. However, I only shook my head and told him, "No. I'm not supposed to leave town while the investigation is open, but since I wasn't planning on going anywhere, that's not a big deal."

"Well, I hope they get it figured out soon." Chuck paused there, expression now sympathetic. "Hazel told me it was your birthday yesterday. How about we take you out for a belated birthday lunch?"

I didn't miss the way he'd said "we." Obviously, some progress had been made while they were off delivering all the solstice celebration leftovers to the Third Street Shelter.

But as much as I appreciated the offer, I didn't think I'd be functional by lunch. "That's really nice of you two," I said. "Can I take a rain check? Right now I'm so tired, I think I just want to go to sleep for the next twelve hours."

"I get it." He'd been smiling slightly, but he turned serious as he asked, "Are you okay to drive back to your place? I can take you, if you want."

"No, that's all right," I replied. The last thing I wanted was to have to come back out to his ranch to get my car. I was here now, and I'd drive it back to my place if it killed me. "It's not far. But thanks."

"If you're sure—"

I assured him I was. In all the hubbub, I'd left my purse behind in his guest bedroom, but he handed it over to me and then offered to follow me back to my apartment, just in case.

Once again, I shot him down...but gently. After Calvin's indifference, it was still nice to have someone around who cared about me, even if it was just as a friend and nothing more.

And at last I climbed wearily behind the wheel of the Beetle and pointed it toward Globe. Maybe my eyelids drooped once or twice, but I managed to make it back to my building without incident. Once there, I parked the car and dragged myself up the stairs, ignoring Archie's recriminations after I got inside the apartment. Yes, I was late, but I'd already warned him I'd be out all night.

I poured some dry food into his bowl and refreshed his water, then stumbled down the hall and went into my room, shutting the door against Archie's grousing. It felt like I was swimming through lead as I removed my shoes and dress, and I could barely keep my eyes open as I slipped into the shower for a quick spritz.

Hair still damp, I put on a clean tank top and panties, and then fell into bed. My eyes shut as soon as my head hit the pillow, but just before sleep reclaimed me, the question continued to swirl in my mind.

Who had killed Lilith Black...and why?

11

Boden My Time

THE BACK DOOR'S BUZZER SEEMED TO ECHO IN my head. I opened one bleary eye and looked at the clock on my bedside table.

Two-fifteen.

Who in the world would be ringing the buzzer at two-fifteen in the morning?

However, as I opened my eyes a little wider, I realized it was dim in my room because of the closed blinds, not because it was dark outside.

Two-fifteen in the afternoon, not in the morning.

Even though it wasn't all that odd a time for someone to be stopping by, I wanted to ignore the buzzer. The sign on the front door of the shop clearly stated that it would be closed until Thursday morning, and I didn't have any deliveries scheduled for that day. Chuck knew I planned to sleep the sleep of the dead, and I assumed he'd probably passed that information along to Hazel.

The buzzer sounded again. I muttered a curse and pushed myself up from the pillows, then stumbled over to the dresser and located a pair of yoga pants. A scrunchie lay in the little bowl on top of the dresser that I used to temporarily store earrings and rings, and I grabbed it and pulled my sleep-mussed hair out of the way.

I doubted I looked at all presentable, but at least I was dressed.

Feet into a pair of handy flip-flops, and then I made my way through the apartment and down the stairs to the back door. I opened it, and saw probably the last person in the world I'd been expecting.

Boden Marsh.

I blinked at him in astonishment…or maybe that was just my reaction to the bright sunlight glaring down on the parking lot outside. "Boden?"

"Can I come in?"

His black hair lay lank on his shoulders, and he was wearing a faded Motorhead T-shirt and jeans rather than the head-to-toe black I'd seen him in previously. And he looked tired, too.

Well, it seemed to be going around.

I realized that it could look pretty bad to be seen with Lilith's former assistant. But there was no one else in the vicinity at the moment, and I really wanted to hear what he had to say.

"Come on in," I told him, moving out of the way so he could step inside.

He entered the micro-foyer, and I went ahead and led him up the stairs to my apartment. Luckily, I'd tidied up after going on my honey-cake baking spree, and so the place was in fairly decent shape.

"Iced tea?" I asked him after I'd closed the door behind us. "I don't know about you, but I could use some caffeine."

"Sounds great."

"Go ahead and sit down in the living room," I said. "I'll meet you there in a sec."

He headed toward the couch. I couldn't help but notice that Archie had positioned himself in an opportune patch of sunlight by the French doors that led to the balcony, but I decided not to try to shoo him out. Doing so would only end badly—and besides, I figured it couldn't hurt to get his input on Boden's story once the cat and I were alone.

I had a big pitcher of sun tea in the fridge, so it didn't take me very long to fill a couple of glasses with ice, then pour the tea over it. In less than a minute, I was in the living room, handing my unexpected guest a glass before settling myself in the armchair that faced the couch.

"Thanks," he said.

"How are you doing?" I asked. Yes, he looked tired and strained, but I couldn't see any real grief in his expression. Maybe the shock of Lilith's death hadn't quite hit him yet.

Or maybe it hadn't affected him all that much because he really didn't care.

Unease swirled through me, and I made myself take a sip of tea. Yes, Calvin had said Boden's alibi was iron-clad...but what if it really wasn't? What if he looked relatively unconcerned about Lilith's murder because he was the one who'd actually committed it?

"I'm okay," Boden said. He also swallowed some tea, then pushed a few strands of limp black hair behind one ear with his free hand. "I mean, I think I'm just still processing all this. I can't believe she's gone."

No, say what you wanted about Lilith Black, but she'd definitely been a larger-than-life presence. When someone like that had their existence snuffed out, their passing did seem to leave a hole in the world.

"I can't, either," I said. "How's Tansy?"

"She's a mess."

I didn't find that too difficult to believe. Although I'd never heard the girl speak a single word, it seemed pretty obvious to me that she practically worshipped the woman who'd been her boss. "And you left her alone?" I asked.

Although I hadn't meant the question as an accusation, Boden stiffened. "She didn't want me around. She said it was my fault that Lilith was dead."

About all I could do in response to such a comment was blink. "Why would she say that?"

Boden's glance slid away from mine. He swallowed some more tea, and wrapped both hands around the glass, its surface now sweating slightly despite my apartment's more than adequate air conditioning. "Because I wasn't with her when— when it happened."

"Where were you?"

Was that a trace of a flush along his cheekbones? I thought it might be; in keeping with his overall goth look, he was very pale, with not even a hint of a tan to hide his natural skin tone.

"I was with a girl I met at the ritual. We went back to her house after it was over."

Ah. Well, that must have been what Calvin had meant by Boden Marsh having an iron-clad alibi. I had no doubt that he'd interviewed the girl involved as well, and she'd confirmed his story that he'd been far away from the scene of the crime when the murder occurred.

And I didn't understand why Boden would

look so hangdog. His personal life was his business. Maybe hooking up with random women at Lilith's various "events" wasn't the most socially responsible behavior, but as long as they were safe, who cared?

A flash of his aura—now dark blue tinged with purple—gave me a bit of a clue. He was embarrassed because he liked me, and he didn't want me to think he was a man-whore.

Honestly, I tried not to judge people's personal lives. As long as everyone involved was a consenting adult, have at it.

I didn't think it would be very politic to tell him that he didn't have a chance in hell with me, and so there was no point in being embarrassed. Instead, I said quietly, "Well, I can see why Tansy might be upset, but unless Lilith hired you specifically to be her bodyguard, I don't think anyone could blame you for what happened."

A look of relief passed over Boden's angular features, and he sat up a little straighter. "No, that definitely wasn't in my job description. She used me to fetch and carry, and to scout locations for her and handle some logistics, but she never felt she needed personal protection."

Misplaced confidence, obviously, although I didn't bother to comment on that.

Before I could say anything, he went on, "Actually she told me she wanted to be alone after the ritual, so I thought it was fine to leave."

I nodded, then said, "Why don't you tell me exactly what happened? Maybe then I can start to get a sense of what might be going on here."

"Because of your own powers?"

Since there was no reason to demur, I nodded. Once I heard the whole story, I might get a flash of insight. Otherwise, I'd consult the Tarot, or visit the crystal ball on the altar in my office and see if Grandma Ellen had any advice she could give me. I figured the quicker I discovered who the real murderer was, the sooner I'd get Calvin Standingbear off my back. Since he obviously had no interest in a personal relationship with me, it seemed the best thing to do was get Lilith Black's murder sorted out so he and I could go our merry ways.

"Okay." Boden swallowed some more tea, then set his glass down on one of the coasters on the coffee table. "The ritual started around nine-thirty. We'd drawn the quarters and set out candles, and there was a bonfire as well."

That all sounded almost exactly like my own ceremony. Which, all right, there were only so many variations on a solstice ritual. Still, I couldn't keep myself from wondering if Lilith or Tansy had spied on my setup and stolen some of my ideas.

"The whole thing lasted for about an hour, I guess," Boden went on. "Well, more, actually, because afterward, people lined up to place their petitions in the bonfire. Lilith presided over the whole thing, waving her hands from time to time to make it look as if she was putting some of her own mojo into the fire."

He paused there and sent me an ironic glance, now looking more like the man who'd spilled all of Lilith's secrets in the produce section of the local Super Walmart. Since I didn't comment, he rubbed his hands on the knees of his jeans before continuing.

"That part probably took another half an hour or so. I think it was around eleven-thirty when the crowd really started to break up. That was when I met Emily."

"The girl with the house?"

"Yeah." He tucked some hair behind the other ear, revealing an impressive row of piercings— hoops and studs and a dangling silver pentacle. "We talked for a while, and she made it pretty clear that she wanted to use some of that midsummer energy with me. She was hot, so I figured, why not?"

About all I could do was make a noncom-mittal sound and take another sip of iced tea. I'd never been the sort of person to indulge in casual sex with people I didn't know, so I couldn't exactly relate.

Even though I was actually the product of exactly that kind of hook-up.

Luckily, my non-response seemed to be enough for Boden, because he went on, "I was with Emily at her house for a few hours, but I decided I didn't want to stay the whole night, so I ducked out a little after five and came back to the Airbnb. There were a bunch of cop cars parked out front, and that's when I found out what had happened."

Personally, I had to wonder if Boden's alibi was as iron-clad as Calvin seemed to think it was. Yes, the coroner had indicated that Lilith had died earlier in the night, but five o'clock was close enough to four that it had to be within the margin of error.

Except, of course, for the fact that there didn't seem to be much of a motive. Even if Lilith and Boden hadn't always gotten along—and I had to admit that I'd never seen them snipe at each other, since she seemed to mostly treat him like part of the furniture—why would he kill the woman who was financing his apparently carefree lifestyle?

"And what about Tansy?" I asked next. "Cal— I mean, Chief Standingbear said she had a good alibi, too."

"Oh, she was working the site with a couple of volunteers, doing clean-up. Tansy and the people who were helping her had been taking some stuff back to the Airbnb when…well, when it happened." Once again, Boden rubbed the palms of his hands on his knees. "She's the one who found Lilith. She was lying next to the remains of the fire with her athame sticking out of her back."

That was the same thing Calvin had told me, but hearing Boden describe it in such a dispassionate way made a little shiver run down my spine. I tried to tell myself that he was handling the situation like this so he wouldn't lose it…and yet I still didn't know for sure. If he really were guilty, wouldn't his aura have looked very different?

Unless the murder truly hadn't left any indelible marks on his soul. I somehow kept myself from shivering at the thought.

To force my mind away from that horrible notion, I said, "Tansy must be very shaken up," and he nodded.

"Yeah, she's taking it pretty hard."

"Shouldn't you be with her?"

Boden stared at me for a second or two, then shook his head, even as a flicker of irritation flashed in his dark eyes. "I doubt it. We don't get along that well."

"Why not?"

A shrug. "Because she could tell I wasn't as convinced by Lilith's all-encompassing greatness as she thought I should be."

Interesting. So, Tansy hadn't realized her idol was a conwoman of the first order?

"She believed in Lilith's powers?" I asked.

Boden let out a disgusted breath. "Oh, yeah. It was kind of sad, actually, but Lilith loved having a little acolyte following her everywhere, worshipping her, so it wasn't as though she would have ever told her the truth."

While all this was interesting, I still couldn't quite see why he'd come to confide in me. Maybe it was simply because I was the only halfway sympathetic person he knew in Globe.

"And so…." I said, drawing out the syllable, not sure if I even knew what I'd meant to say.

"You're wondering why I came to see you."

"Frankly, yes."

He didn't look offended. Actually, a faint smile touched his mouth. "Because I want to know what really happened. I'm sorry you got dragged into the situation—Tansy told me that Chief Standingbear questioned you—but I know you're innocent…and I also know you're probably the only person in Globe who can get to the bottom of all this."

I wanted to thank Boden for his vote of confidence, but I wasn't so sure. True, I had a plan to reach out to my higher powers to see if I could determine who had killed Lilith Black, and yet I hadn't intended to tell anyone about that plan. I figured I'd try quietly on my own, and if that didn't work out, I'd go on to Plan B. But with Boden asking me for help, he'd know right away if I failed miserably.

Which, I reminded myself, wasn't the end of the world. Magic, as I was so fond of pointing out, wasn't what you could call an exact science. Sometimes the spirit world came at your call, and sometimes it pretended you didn't exist.

"I'm not so sure about that…." I began slowly, and he shook his head.

"Well, I am. I heard how you were able to discover who really killed Lucien Dumond. Why should this be any different?"

Because unless the killer shows up in my apartment and tips his or her hand, I doubt it's going to be that easy, I thought. The only reason why Eugene Dershowitz and Violet Clarke hadn't killed me outright was because they needed me to talk to Lucien's ghost and find out where he'd hidden his will. In the end, the joke was on them, since he'd left almost everything to me anyway. Still, I didn't think this was remotely the same type of situation.

I could have pointed all that out to Boden Marsh, but I refrained. The particulars of the story hadn't made the rounds, and I preferred to keep it that way.

"I'll see what I can do," I said.

"Great," Boden responded, clearly not put off by my less than enthusiastic answer. "I thought we could go to the place where she was killed, see if we can pick up any vibes."

Oh, boy. Although I'd done pretty much the same thing while trying to investigate Lucien's death, I didn't know if it was such a good idea this particular go-'round. If Calvin caught me snooping around down there....

"I'm not sure it's wise to interfere with an active crime scene," I said, and my guest deflated, slumping against the back of the couch.

However, he seemed to perk up as he said, "I don't think it's active anymore. Chief Standing-bear told Tansy and me that we could go back after noon today to clear out the rest of the stuff that got left behind, so that has to mean it's okay to take a look, right?"

If that was really what Calvin had said, then I supposed it would be all right. I could see how the San Ramon tribe would want the area opened up and the detritus from Lilith's ritual removed as soon as possible.

However, I also knew that if Boden really wanted me to poke around and pick up on the vibes in the crime scene, I needed to go alone. It was hard enough sensing that sort of thing when I was by myself; I knew if I had someone else around—especially someone I didn't know very well—then my chances of discovering anything useful would be much lower.

"Maybe," I said. "But—and don't take this the wrong way—I have to go alone. It's hard for me to do this sort of work with an audience."

His face fell. I could tell that he really wanted to go with me. Because he was just that eager to get to the bottom of the mystery, or because he'd been hoping for some alone time for the two of us?

I was probably flattering myself.

To my relief, though, he didn't seem inclined to push it. He tapped his fingers against his knees, almost as if trying out some sort of staccato rhythm. Since he used to be a drummer, it was probably an unconscious tic.

Then he said, "I guess I can understand that. Are you sure it's safe?"

Very good question. I wanted to believe that Lilith's killer had a grudge against her personally, and so I wouldn't be in any kind of danger to go poking around the clearing where she'd died. However, there was also a chance that the person —or persons—involved were still lurking in the area, and would do whatever it took to ensure that the crime remained unsolved.

My skin prickled. Getting stabbed in the back was not how I wanted to leave this world, even if I knew that something more waited for me on the other side. Death was really nothing to be scared of.

Pain, on the other hand....

"I don't know," I said frankly. "But it's a risk I'm willing to take. Also, I'll consult my spirit guides before I go, see if they have any words of wisdom for me. And I'll bring along my pepper spray."

The pepper spray was a relic of my time living along in Los Angeles. I'd never had any reason to use it, but a girl couldn't be too careful.

That comment seemed to relax Boden, because he shifted backward slightly on the couch and gave me a nod. "Well, then. I suppose you've thought of everything."

I wished. In my experience, it was usually the one angle you hadn't considered that nailed you in the end.

But I didn't say anything on that subject. No, I just smiled and said, "I hope so. Why don't you give me your number? I'll call or text if I come up with anything."

He seemed pleased that I'd asked him for his phone number. At least, the corners of his mouth lifted slightly as he rattled off the digits.

Since I had my phone with me, it was easy enough to create a new contact entry for him. While I had my head bent over the phone, I had to hope he wasn't reading anything more into the request than there was. He might have spent a night with one of Lilith's groupies, but it didn't seem as if she'd left a lasting impression on him.

After that, though, there wasn't much to do except make another promise to let Boden know as soon as I found something, and then walk him to the door. Once there, he paused and gave me a searching look.

"I really appreciate you doing this," he said, and his tone was a little too warm, too intimate, for my comfort.

"Pure self-interest," I responded lightly. I needed to nip his intentions—whatever they were —right in the bud. "I have to live in this town. I don't want everyone thinking I'm a murderer."

"I know you're not," he said, still doing his best to hold my gaze.

"So do I—but I have a lot of work to do," I told him. "Hang in there, and I'll be in touch."

To my infinite relief, he accepted the dismissal for what it was. He tilted his head at me, said a casual goodbye, and headed down the stairs.

I closed the door and leaned my head against it...and wondered if my life could get any more complicated.

Famous last words....

12

Pack Mentality

I HADN'T BEEN LYING TO BODEN WHEN I TOLD him I had a lot of work to do. Although I realized that I'd probably have to end up in the clearing at one point or another, I needed to lay some groundwork first.

Well, first I actually had to respond to a series of texts from Hazel that I'd noticed when I unlocked my phone and entered Boden's contact info. Obviously, she was worried that I was already locked up and awaiting trial or something.

I'm okay, I wrote back. *Calvin asked me some questions, but I'm not under arrest or anything. Right now I'm just trying to figure out what really happened. I'll be in touch.*

She probably would have liked more details than that, but for the time being, it should be enough to let her know Calvin hadn't shoved me in a jail cell and thrown away the key.

After that, I went into the office to get one of my Tarot decks. As I entered, Archie, who'd been sleeping in the little cubby under the desk, opened an annoyed golden eye and said, "Your boyfriend gone?"

"He's not my boyfriend," I replied. "He's someone I know who needs help. You really need to stop seeing boyfriends in every tree."

"Mixed metaphor," he said crisply. Although he'd never told me much about his life before being turned into a cat, I sometimes wondered if Archie had been an English teacher or something back when he was human. He definitely had a pedantic streak that seemed guaranteed to pluck my last nerve.

"Whatever," I muttered, ignoring the way Archie put his nose in the air and flounced from the room.

Good. I always worked better when I was alone.

I went over to the low bookcase on one wall and opened the carved wooden box that held my two favorite Tarot decks. Since this was about dark business, I opted for the Crow deck rather than the whimsical Everyday Witch one, since that particular deck was generally better suited for questions about love and prosperity, not trying to get clues as to who had murdered someone in your orbit.

Not that choosing the correct deck for the task at hand seemed to help much. I went over to my altar and did a simple three-card spread, and all I got was a muddle of minor arcana cards that didn't seem to offer much in the way of illumination.

Well, sometimes it took a couple of tries to get a useful result.

However, after doing three more spreads and getting similar responses, I shuffled the Crow deck and put it back in the box, and got out my Everyday Witch cards.

No soap. The responses were even worse, if possible.

I suppose I could have gone through all fifteen of my decks—yes, I was a Tarot deck hoarder, sue me—but I already knew that if the universe wasn't vibing to a particular means of divination, it was time to move on.

My pendulum and a bag of runes sat on my altar, and yet I decided there wasn't much point in consulting them, either. No, it was obviously time to move on to the big guns.

I reached for the crystal ball on its heavy wooden stand and settled it closer to me. Thank the Goddess, it had survived being flung at Eugene Dershowitz without suffering any lasting damage except a couple of very small nicks. I had no reason to believe I'd have any trouble contacting Grandma Ellen with a new crystal ball, but frankly, enough of my life was still new and strange. I didn't want to deal with breaking in a new crystal ball on top of everything else.

For a moment, I allowed myself to sit quietly, to put the tumult of the past twenty-four hours behind me so I could achieve the mental stillness necessary for spirit work. True, my grandmother tended to pop up in the crystal ball without a lot of effort on my part, and yet I still thought it was a good idea to keep up the routine, just so I wouldn't lapse into any bad habits.

Then I focused on the image of my mother's mother, a woman who would always remain perpetually pretty and in her early forties because of her untimely death from uterine cancer. Not that she ever seemed particularly troubled that her mortal life had been cut short; she appeared to be just fine with the afterlife she was currently living.

Her face appeared in the crystal ball, blue eyes a shade or two lighter than mine fixed on me, blonde hair waving around her oval face. "Selena," she said. "It seems that tragedy has fallen on your little town yet again."

I didn't ask her how she knew what had happened to Lilith Black. The spirits in the summerlands generally seemed to have a pretty good idea of what was going on in the mortal plane, even if they weren't exactly what you could call omniscient and were definitely detached from the drama of human life.

"Unfortunately, yes," I replied. "The Tarot isn't giving me much to work with. I was hoping you might have some insights."

She closed her eyes for a moment. While I doubted she would come right out and tell me who had murdered Lilith Black, I still hoped she could point me in the right direction to find the clues that would solve the mystery.

The crystal ball remained cool under my hands. Sometimes it warmed to my touch, but not that day. Since there didn't seem to be much rhyme or reason to the sensation, I'd come to believe it didn't mean a whole heck of a lot.

Grandma Ellen's lashes—thick and dark—lifted, and she stared straight at me. "You need to go to the clearing at nine o'clock tonight. If you do that, you'll find the answers you seek."

"Why nine o'clock?" I asked, although I knew it generally wasn't a good idea to question a spirit guide's utterances…even if the spirit guide in question was your own grandmother. Honestly, I wasn't thrilled about the thought of wandering around alone in the dark in a place where two people had met violent ends. Even though I knew Lucien's ghost was long gone, that didn't mean

Lilith's spirit might not be lurking around somewhere. And I sort of doubted she'd be in a good mood.

At any rate, it seemed much safer to head over there during full daylight. Much less chance of getting ambushed that way.

"Nine o'clock," my grandmother repeated, her tone almost sharp. She sounded like a woman letting her child know what would happen if they kept offering her any sass.

"All right," I said wearily. Might as well admit defeat. It just wasn't smart to go against advice from your spirit guide. "Nine o'clock it is. You want to tell me why?"

Her eyes narrowed, but the quirk of her pink lipsticked mouth seemed to speak of some secret amusement. "I already told you. That's how you'll find the answer you've been seeking."

And she winked out, leaving the crystal ball clear and empty.

Great. I suppose I could have pleaded with her to return and give me more clarification, but I had a feeling that would just make her cranky. Once a spirit had made her pronouncement, she really didn't like to be disturbed.

Okay, then. I'd head out at a little before nine o'clock, and I'd make sure I was armed with my pepper spray and a walking stick I'd bought at Odds and Ends, a store down the street that sold a little bit of everything, including hiking supplies. The stick was a sturdy piece of burnished oak with a raven carved near the top—it had been made by Lou Foster, a local artisan—and I figured it would do well enough as a weapon in a pinch if my pepper spray failed me.

Now all I had to do was wait for the fateful hour.

As I drove away from my apartment, Globe was sleepy and dark; the place wasn't known for being a party town, especially on a Wednesday night. Archie had asked a couple of questions, but since I'd been there to feed him and make sure the schedule was maintained, he didn't seem too worried about me wandering around in the woods after dark.

"Try not to get yourself killed. It would be most inconvenient," he said, then curled up on the seat of my favorite armchair.

That was probably a display of affection...for him. Or he was just worried about who would feed him if I ended up getting axe-murdered in the pursuit of truth.

The moon was up, though, nearly full and shining brightly enough that I probably could have gotten by without the flashlight I'd brought along. I parked as close to the spot as I could manage, noting how the ground showed the dusty tracks of multiple tires, and the way the grass had been crushed by the pressure of hundreds of feet. Hopefully, the area wouldn't take too long to bounce back, especially once we started getting those mythical summer monsoon storms.

I'd put on jeans and my hiking boots, so I figured I should be set for poking around. Honestly, I didn't know much about investigating a crime scene, although I told myself that wasn't really the point. Calvin and his deputies had already been out here and hadn't found a single piece of useful evidence. No, I was here to discover the things that couldn't be seen with the naked eye, to try my best to pick up the vibrations of violence. The idea was a little unsettling, but I'd been through something similar before.

Once again, though, I had to hope I wouldn't encounter Lilith's ghost. Lucien's howling, barely intelligible shade had been bad enough during our first meeting…and he'd actually been kindly disposed toward me. An overtly hostile spirit would be an order of magnitude worse.

Fighting back a shiver, I moved through the trees, dead leaves crunching under the tread of my hiking boots. The sound seemed far too loud, and I did my best to lighten my step, even as I wondered if my heart was beating hard enough for anyone—or anything—else to hear.

As I'd expected, the clearing was empty. At the center lay the remains of the bonfire, not much left to mark the spot except a ring of stones and a couple of mostly consumed logs. I wondered why Boden and Tansy hadn't come back to get rid of the detritus, since it sounded as though the San Ramon tribe wanted the place cleared out as soon as possible.

Maybe Boden had decided to wait until I'd finished my own investigation, fearing that any disruption of the site might make it harder for me to pick up the vibrations there.

Speaking of which....

I paused a foot or so away from the fire and pulled in a breath. The faint scent of wood smoke seemed to still hang in the air, and underneath that I could smell the mossy dampness of the river a few yards away, and something drifting on the wind that might have been dry grass, still warm after baking in the sun all day.

The back of my neck tingled, although I couldn't really feel anything here. It wasn't like the time when Lucien's spirit had stirred up the wind and tugged at my hair. No, this particular night felt almost deadly still, although underneath the quiet, I could somehow sense the wrongness of the place. Too many deaths in this spot, I supposed.

When this was all over, someone needed to come back here and smudge the living crud out of the place.

The faintest rustle of dead leaves reached my ears, and I sidled over to a cottonwood tree, slipping behind it even as one hand tightened on the walking stick it held and the other gripped the pepper spray I'd slipped into one pocket.

Was the killer returning to the scene of the crime?

Cold inched its way down my spine as I realized what had made that sound.

A big coyote, ears pricked up and tail held at attention, entered the clearing. It paused for a moment, seeming to survey its surroundings, and then began sniffing around the remains of the campfire.

Could it smell me?

I had no idea, since I'd never done much research on coyotes' olfactory acuity. The animals had been in short supply in my neighborhood in West L.A., although I knew they could be a real problem to anyone who lived on the edge of California's wilderness areas. Or even not so wild— they'd been spotted multiple times in Griffith Park and Runyon Canyon, both locations that weren't exactly out in the middle of nowhere.

But the spot where I stood wasn't located someplace relatively safe, like Griffith Park. If that coyote figured out I was here and decided to attack, all I had to protect myself was a walking stick and some pepper spray, both of which seemed pretty flimsy at the moment.

The coyote continued to sniff its way around, seemingly oblivious to my presence. I held my breath as best I could and hoped it would realize there was no prey here, no rabbit or packrat or whatever else it might have been looking for as its midnight snack.

After a moment, the coyote shook. A sign of annoyance?

I didn't know, since it was facing away from me. Coyotes weren't exactly my field of expertise, and I'd never had a dog growing up, since most of the apartments where my mother and I had lived didn't allow them as pets.

And then....

The coyote shook again, and then seemed to shiver, and bulge...and grow.

Upward, upward, shifting from four legs to two legs. The grayish-dun fur transformed into smooth brown skin and shining dark hair, pulled back into a tight ponytail.

The coyote was Calvin Standingbear.

A startled gasp escaped my lips, and he immediately turned toward me. The moonlight was bright enough that I could see the way his eyes narrowed.

"Selena," he said, sounding almost resigned, as if he somehow understood that he couldn't have escaped the moment when I learned the truth about him, no matter how hard he tried to keep me at arm's length.

He was wearing jeans and a dark T-shirt and boots. Where they'd come from, I had no idea. They'd just sort of…appeared.

"Um, hi, Calvin," I replied as I stepped out from the shelter of my tree.

"What are you doing here?"

"Investigating," I said. An awkward silence hung in the air for a second or two. But since there was no way to ignore what I'd just seen, I asked, "Do you want to tell me what all that was about?"

"Not really." His mouth pressed into a hard line, and he shook his head. "You weren't supposed to see that."

"But I did see it," I returned. "What, are you some kind of were-coyote?"

At once, he shook his head. "That's not what we call ourselves. We're shapeshifters, nothing more."

Nothing more. I'd say that was enough on its own. I also realized he'd said "we," and asked,

"You mean all of the San Ramon Apaches are shifters?"

"Yes." Just that one hard syllable, as if he'd realized it was pointless to lie to me but still hated the necessity of telling the truth.

No wonder they kept to themselves. Realization dawned in me...along with hope, even as I told myself not to get too excited. "This is why you dumped me? Because you couldn't tell me that you were a coyote shifter?"

He winced slightly at the word "dumped"...but he didn't try to deny it, either. "Yes. We're forbidden to get involved with anyone outside the tribe."

"Well, that's a silly rule," I remarked, and Calvin's brows drew together.

"I don't see what's so 'silly' about it."

"I do," I said. I slipped the pepper spray back into my pocket and laid down the walking stick, then moved closer. The whole time, he watched me with wary dark eyes, as if I were the wild animal and he the human I was stalking. "You could have just told me the truth, you know. I'm a witch—I'm used to the strange and unusual."

"There's 'strange and unusual,' and then there's this."

Stopping a foot or so away from him seemed the safest choice. I didn't want to push things too hard. "Can you control it?"

"What?"

"Your shapeshifting."

Something about the hard set of his shoulders seemed to relax ever so slightly. However, his expression remained wary as he said, "Yes. We're not werewolves—we don't have to fear the full moon, and we control the change. It's better if we shift at least once each month, because otherwise, we begin to lose touch with that side of ourselves, but it's still always under our control."

Those words reassured me. All right, I thought I was doing pretty well with accepting the knowledge that the man I lusted after wasn't entirely human, but still, it was good to know that I didn't have to worry about him busting out with the fur and the claws while standing in the checkout line at Walmart.

"Then I really don't see what the problem is," I said as he stared at me in astonishment. "I mean, we all have sides of ourselves that we don't like to talk about."

"This isn't a gambling addiction or a fascination with game shows, you know," Calvin replied, now sounding somewhat strangled.

"I know that," I told him. "Still, I don't think it's as big a deal as you're making it out to be, either. You could have told me. It would have been fine."

"It's not that simple."

And okay, I got that part of it. The San Ramon tribe had a very good reason for keeping this part of themselves secret from the rest of the world. On the other hand, I liked to think that I wasn't "the rest of the world." I was a practicing witch with powers of my own, not a prosy CPA or something. Obviously, Calvin's people didn't have much experience with witches and their tendency to be extremely open-minded when it came to the supernatural.

True, there was that long-ago witch in Globe who'd cursed Archie to be a cat, but I had no reason to believe she would have had much inter-action with the San Ramon Apache. The world had been a much more segregated place sixty years earlier.

"Because you're *making* it difficult," I said. "Don't you have free will? Do you have to do everything your tribe tells you to do?"

He hesitated, expression taut, worried. At the same time, I thought I could see the yearning in his eyes.

And that told me he hadn't wanted to walk away. He'd only been following the rules laid down by his people, and I told myself I couldn't be too angry with him over that.

But as far as I was concerned, some rules were made to be broken.

"I already know the worst," I went on. "Or at

least, what some people might consider to be the worst. And I honestly don't care. I'm also very good at keeping secrets. No one will ever find out because of me."

Calvin's hands clenched into fists. Even in the moonlight, I could see the muscles standing out on his arms. This had to be unbelievably difficult. As much as I wanted to step toward him and wrap my arms around him, I knew I needed to stay put. He knew how I felt, and now he had to decide what to do about it.

Then he said, "I think you're going to get me into a lot of trouble," right before he closed the distance between us with one quick stride and pulled me into his arms.

That kiss was everything I'd hoped for and more—strong…passionate…tasting faintly of mint, which made me wonder if he'd been chewing gum before he turned into a coyote to scout the crime scene—the kind of kiss that made sweet waves of warmth flow all through my body. The clearing spun around me, all moonlight and dappled leaves and cool night air, and I clung to him, knowing he'd hold me up, wouldn't allow my suddenly weak knees to let me collapse to the ground.

It could have been a century, or only a couple of minutes. I didn't know, and I supposed it didn't really matter. What mattered was that I was pretty sure I never wanted to kiss anyone except Calvin Standingbear for the rest of my life.

He seemed a little overwhelmed, too; as he pulled a few inches away, shock and wonder flared in his night-dark eyes. When he spoke, though, his tone was almost rueful.

"Now I know why I was trying to avoid you."

"Excuse me?" I returned. How in the world could he view that kiss as anything except utterly amazing?

"I somehow sensed that our chemistry would be combustible."

Oh. Well, then, I suppose I could understand why he'd felt the need to back off. No point in lighting a fire when you knew you'd have to immediately put it out.

I snuggled against his chest, heard the strong, steady beat of his heart...felt the rock-hard firmness of his body beneath my cheek. "And what did you get for avoiding the unavoidable?" I asked. "Two wasted months."

He chuckled. "Better than two years."

True. I lifted my head and gazed up at him. "And you're not going to take off on me again?"

"No," he replied, even as his arms tightened around me. "I have absolutely no idea how I'm going to explain this to my family, but...."

"I don't see why you have to 'explain' anything," I said firmly. "You're a grown man, and

I'm a grown woman. And you're a shifter, and I'm a witch. It's all fine."

"I'm not sure the tribal elders will accept that logic, but okay." A caressing brush of his hand over my hair, and then he released me, taking a step back. "I'll deal with them later."

I decided to let it go. After all, he'd clearly made the choice to be with me...and that choice had to have been a difficult one. I'd never been part of a close-knit family and community the way Calvin was, and so I didn't have much frame of reference when it came to living my life against other people's wishes.

What I'd told him was the truth, though. I'd never betray his secret, would take it with me to the grave.

"So...what now?" I asked, and he bent and kissed me again, more gently this time, before he straightened once more and glanced around the clearing.

"We solve this crime," he said.

13

Backstabbers

RIGHT. CALVIN AND I HAD BOTH COME TO the clearing with the same purpose in mind—to discover Lilith Black's killer.

"I didn't sense a darn thing," I said, my tone now plaintive, and he smiled and shook his head.

"I couldn't pick up anything, either," he replied. "Or at least, nothing specific. There's the scent of lots of different people here, but trying to tease out any one individual feels almost impossible."

Frowning a little, I stepped away from him and walked clockwise around the remains of the bonfire, hoping that maybe if I trod the same path as those who'd been here the night before, I might be able to pick up something of their energy. After I'd made my circuit, I paused and glanced over at Calvin.

"Still nothing," I said. "I can't believe I'm saying this, but I almost wish this place really was haunted by Lilith's ghost. At least that way, I could talk to her and maybe get some answers."

"She's definitely not here?"

"Not that I can tell." I tucked a strand of hair behind my ear and looked around once again. "It's always really difficult to say who will move on to the next plane and who'll get stuck on this one. Sudden, violent death isn't always the key. Even when people lose their life that way, they don't always stick around."

Calvin seemed to absorb that piece of information, his own forehead puckered with a frown. "Any theories as to why Lilith seems to have moved on so quickly when Lucien didn't?"

"Not really," I admitted. "I mean, I suppose it could be something as simple as him having actual power and her being a total fraud. His will was strong enough to keep him anchored here, since he desperately wanted to communicate to me who his killers were."

"It's still kind of amazing to think she was faking the whole thing," Calvin said. "All those followers. You'd think one of them would've been able to see through her act."

I shrugged. "People believe what they want to believe. All it takes is someone telling them the story they want to hear, and they're willing to suspend a heck of a lot of disbelief. So many people desperately want to believe that witchcraft —magic—will come along and cure all their ills. It's just not that simple, though."

He gave a faint nod, as if absorbing my comments. "But it's real, isn't it?"

"Oh, yes." There might have been a lot of things in the world I wasn't entirely certain about, but magic definitely wasn't one of them. "It's not always as showy as some people want to think, but it exists." I paused there and slanted a look up at him. "I'm surprised you'd be even a little skeptical, considering—"

"Considering I'm a coyote shifter?" he cut in, grinning so his teeth flashed in the moonlight. "I guess I can see why you'd think there might be a bit of cognitive dissonance there. I suppose the whole shifter thing has been a part of my people's history for so long that I don't really think of it as magic. It's just…what is."

"How did it happen?" I asked next, genuinely curious. After all, an entire tribe of people who could change their forms and morph into coyotes wasn't exactly the sort of thing you ran into every day.

"The legends say that one of the San Ramon Apaches' chiefs fell asleep in the lair of a coyote one night while out hunting, but we don't really know for sure." Calvin looked away from me then, gazing off into the distance, as if searching for that long-forgotten spot. "It was many, many years ago, long before the colonizers came to this continent."

So, at least five hundred years. I had to remind myself that Calvin's people had lived on this same land for generation upon generation. Back then, they wouldn't have called themselves the San Ramon Apaches, since even I knew that was a name bestowed upon them by their Spanish conquerors.

Well, whenever and however it had happened, clearly, the San Ramon people had learned to live with their peculiar talent. At the moment, I was just glad that Calvin had decided not to allow it to be a barrier between us anymore.

And, as he'd said a few minutes earlier, we had a crime to solve. I was very, very glad that he'd said "we"; unlike the case of Lucien's murder, Calvin didn't seem inclined to tell me to butt out this time.

Probably because he knew I wouldn't listen anyway.

"I wish we had something more to go on," I said, and his expression hardened, signaling that he'd recognized the change of subject.

"I do, too." He looked around the clearing, then let out a disgusted-sounding breath. "But there were just too many people in this spot recently to have any one individual come through clearly. Same problem when we first swept the crime scene—there were so many footprints, so much physical evidence like cigarette butts and discarded tickets, that kind of thing, that I doubt we'll be able to make much sense of it. My deputies took all the evidence back to the station to have it analyzed, but I have a feeling we won't find much."

I nodded, then glanced around as well. It sounded as though the crowds at Lilith's ritual had left behind something of a mess, but clearly, Calvin's deputies—and then Tansy and whoever she'd brought with her to finish cleaning up the place—had made sure there wasn't much remaining to clutter the scene.

And I seemed to be having the devil of a time picking up any useful vibrations. This sort of thing had happened to me before, so I knew I couldn't force it. Sometimes I could walk into a house and practically hear an argument someone had had there the day before, and other times I couldn't feel anything more than any regular person might. With focus and meditation, I'd managed to strengthen my psychic powers over the years, but they weren't foolproof, by any stretch of the imagination.

"Well, it looks like this place isn't going to give us anything useful," I said, and didn't bother to keep the disappointment out of my tone. I couldn't even be irritated with Grandma Ellen's advice, since all she'd said was that I would find the answer I was seeking. At the time, I'd thought she was referring to the mystery of Lilith Black's death. Now, of course, I realized she'd really been talking about the question of why Calvin had walked away from our budding relationship.

It wasn't an answer I'd expected, but I could live with it…especially since it looked as though things between us were back on course.

I was just about to add that we might as well leave and try coming back in the daytime—not that I thought a bit of sunshine would provide any more clues than what we'd already found—when a sudden flash of an image appeared in my mind. It was so unexpected that I clapped my hand to my forehead and winced.

"Are you okay, Selena?" Calvin asked, taking a step toward me. Even in the uncertain moonlight, I could see the worry in his expression.

"I'm fine," I said. "I just picked up something."

"What?"

For a moment, I didn't reply. The vision had come and gone so quickly that I didn't have much of chance to pick out too many details.

"Lilith, standing over there." I pointed toward a spot a few feet away from the remnants of the midsummer bonfire. "She was arguing with a man."

"Boden Marsh?" Calvin asked immediately.

A logical response, I supposed, alibi or no.

However, I knew that wasn't who I'd seen in the vision. "No, this man had brown hair, not black, and it was cut short. He was tall, though—enough taller than Lilith that he was staring down into her face. It must have been after everyone else had left, because I didn't see anyone but the two of them in my vision."

"The initial report from the M.E. seems to indicate she was stabbed by someone a lot taller than she was, based on the angle of the wounds and where the knife was found in her back," Calvin responded, tone musing. "Maybe you saw her killer. You said they were arguing. What were they saying?"

All I could do was give a helpless shrug. "Sorry, I didn't hear anything. I'm just guessing from the expressions on their faces that they were having an argument. The man was scowling, and she was frowning, too, and had her hands on her hips."

"Anything else? Any details about the guy?"

I didn't answer directly, and instead closed my eyes and willed my brain to conjure up the image once again. Yes, there was the man—the lighting made it hard for me to tell for sure, but I thought he was probably a few years older than Lilith, in his late thirties. He wore a dress shirt and what appeared to be nice trousers, not the sort of outfit most people would choose for attending a pagan ritual in the woods. Was that an Apple watch strapped on his wrist, just above where his hands were jammed into the pockets of his slacks?

Dutifully, I related all these details to Calvin, and a frown of his own pulled the straight black brows together. "Whatever they were talking about, it doesn't sound very amicable," he said. "I don't suppose you've seen anyone who looked like this guy hanging around Globe lately?"

I shook my head. "No, but I spent a lot of time the past couple of days getting ready for my own ritual, so I wasn't exactly 'hanging out.' No one like that came into my store to get a ticket to my ceremony, though. I know that much."

"I had a feeling, but I thought I might as well ask." He was silent for a moment, obviously thinking things over. "Still, it's a good piece of information. Tomorrow morning we can go talk to Tansy, give her the guy's description and see if she knows who he is."

I wanted to ask why we should wait, but I thought I already knew the answer. Although I wasn't wearing a watch, I knew it was probably close to ten o'clock. While I supposed if the matter was urgent enough, Calvin would go ahead and see Lilith's assistant no matter what time it was, I had a feeling he'd decided to put the interview off until the morning because he honestly didn't know whether this lead truly meant anything or not.

Unfortunately, neither did I. Just because the man had been arguing with Lilith didn't meant he was the one who'd stuck a ceremonial dagger in her back.

And again, I was just reassured that Calvin had said "we," and wasn't going to give me any nonsense about this being official police business and something I needed to stay out of.

"Okay," I said. "Pick me up at ten?"

"Sounds like a plan," he replied. Even better, he bent and kissed me again, a good, solid kiss that sent tingles all the way to my toes and reminded me once again that I couldn't imagine being with anyone except him.

He walked me back to my car, and watched for a moment as I drove off. As he disappeared in my rearview mirror, I smiled.

Everything was going better than I could have possibly imagined.

The next morning, Calvin was promptly at the back door to my building at 10 a.m. This time, though, he was in full uniform, signaling that this was definitely an official errand. Because I'd already guessed his jeans wouldn't make a reappearance, I'd put on one of my pretty skirts from India and a scoop-neck T-shirt, although the day already promised to be hot enough that a tank top might have been a better choice.

I got in the passenger seat of his official SUV and adjusted my sunglasses on my nose. "Are you sure Tansy will even be there?" I asked as we pulled out of the parking lot that backed up to the shop.

His gaze remained fixed on the road. "She's already been told not to leave town. And she also said she had no plans to go anywhere until the coroner's office releases Lilith's body."

"Tansy's taking care of the funeral arrangements?" Somehow, I had a hard time visualizing that pale, silent girl doing anything so practical.

"Apparently. She said that Lilith hasn't spoken to her family in years, so she'll be handling everything."

I absorbed that comment and nodded. Something about learning that Lilith was estranged from her family made me a little sad. My own mother still didn't quite understand the whole witch thing, but she also had never tried to stop me from pursuing my dream. We still chatted every week, sometimes on the phone, sometimes via a Zoom meeting, depending on what else she was doing that day.

Honestly, I didn't even know for sure where exactly Lilith called home. Because her schtick involved traveling around the country and performing rituals in various "powerful" locales, all her videos seemed to be filmed in various Airbnbs or other vacation homes.

We headed up Mesquite Street, going toward the Airbnb that Josie's friend Muriel owned and where Lilith and her entourage had been staying while in Globe. As we approached the little bungalow—painted a cheerful yellow with dark green trim—a man came hurrying out of the house. He was tall, with brown hair several shades lighter than Calvin's coal-black locks, and he wore a dress shirt and slacks. Even as we slowed down and began to pull up to the curb, the man climbed into a Mercedes coupe parked in the short driveway in front of the one-car garage and began to back out.

"Is that...?" Calvin asked, and I nodded.

"I think so."

He pushed down on the gas pedal, clearly intending to block the driveway. With a screech of brakes, the Mercedes came to an abrupt halt, just inches away from crashing into the front fender of Calvin's Durango.

"Got you," Calvin said with grim satisfaction, and unbuckled his seat belt and got out.

I followed suit, barely avoiding tripping over my long skirt as I jumped out of the SUV. He was already standing by the driver-side door of the Mercedes, which I vaguely noted had California plates.

"Mind getting out of the vehicle, sir?"

The door opened, and the brown-haired man got out. He was good-looking in a spray-tanned, L.A. sort of way, and appeared very out of place on this street of vintage houses and older-model vehicles.

"Just what the hell is this about?" the man demanded.

You'd think the uniform would've been enough, but—showing more patience than I probably would have—Calvin also pulled his I.D. out of his pocket and flashed it at the guy. "Calvin Standingbear, San Ramon tribal police. I'm investigating Lilith Black's murder. And you are?"

"Doug Snyder," the brown-haired man replied. "I'm Lilith's business manager."

Well, that explained why the two of them had been arguing in my vision. Or at least, it explained how they knew one another.

"Got it," Calvin said. "Let's all go inside and discuss what you're doing in Globe."

For a second, Doug stared at Calvin, clearly

wondering if he should protest. But then he seemed to take in all six feet, four inches of the police chief's looming form and decide that maybe putting up any kind of resistance probably wasn't such a good idea.

"Fine," he said, although the word came out almost as a snarl.

The three of us headed up the front walk, and Calvin knocked on the door. It opened almost at once, and Tansy stared out at us in surprise. "Doug?" she managed, in a wispy little voice that matched her appearance perfectly. "Um...what?"

"We need to come in and have a talk," Calvin said, and Tansy's blue-gray eyes widened even further.

"Oh...okay."

She stepped out of the way, and the three of us trooped inside. The place wasn't very big, but had been furnished in a lively cottage style with lots of blue and yellow and green, matching the exterior of the house perfectly. Almost immediately inside the front door was the living room, and Calvin pointed at the overstuffed couch.

"You can go ahead and sit down," he said. The words were phrased politely enough, but the steel underlying his tone indicated he wouldn't take no for an answer.

Doug Snyder didn't offer any protests, but went to the sofa and sat down on the middle cushion. Still looking mystified—and a little scared—Tansy seated herself as well, although on a hard-backed side chair a few feet away.

Since I was with Calvin, I figured I'd better remain standing. Even though it had been my vision that had sent us here, I knew he was the one conducting the investigation, and so I'd let him take the lead…for the moment, anyway.

"So," he went on, now sounding almost casual, as if he had his suspects right where he wanted them and therefore could relax a bit. "Why don't you tell me what you're doing here, Mr. Snyder?"

"Like I told you before, I'm Lilith Black's business manager," Doug said. He looked more annoyed than anything else, as if he'd been interrupted on his way to get coffee or something, rather than detained for questioning in a murder investigation. "I always accompany her on these trips. I got hung up with some business in L.A., though, so I drove out yesterday afternoon." He paused there, and squinted up at Calvin. "That's all you need to know."

Not even a blink in response to the other man's snotty tone. "Oh, I'll be the one to decide what I 'need to know,'" Calvin responded. "And it's probably a good idea if you cooperate, Mr. Snyder. If you don't want to talk here, I can always put you under arrest and take you to the station for questioning. I guarantee that won't be nearly as comfortable as what we're doing now."

Doug Snyder's spray tan wouldn't exactly allow him to turn pale, although he did look a little pinched around the nose and mouth. "Under arrest for what?"

"For the murder of Lilith Black," Calvin said easily. "A witness saw you arguing with her only a few hours before her death. Care to explain what that was about?"

I guessed that he'd made the statement about there being a witness because he wanted to put Doug Snyder off balance. At the same time, I had to wonder if a psychic vision would be admissible as evidence in court. I noticed how Calvin hadn't said who that witness was, or how they'd managed to see an argument Doug probably had thought was private.

For some reason, Doug and Tansy exchanged a single uneasy glance. But then he said, "Nothing."

"It didn't look like nothing."

Dead silence for a couple of seconds. Then Tansy knotted her thin fingers in her black-clad lap and said in her little-girl voice, "It was about me."

Calvin's head swiveled toward her. "How so?"

She bit her lip. Right then, she looked about sixteen years old. In that same wispy, almost breathless tone, she replied, "Lilith found out that Doug and I were in a relationship."

I could feel my eyebrows go shooting up. All right, I knew that Tansy was probably in her early twenties and older than she looked, but still. There had to be at least fifteen years separating her and Doug Snyder, maybe more.

Lilith's manager thrust out his jaw, looking belligerent. "Yes, we were. And it was none of Lilith's business."

"I assume Lilith thought otherwise," Calvin observed, a glint that was almost amused entering his dark eyes.

"Yes," Tansy put in before Doug could reply. "Lilith always wanted all the focus to be on her. She didn't want anyone who worked with her to have any kind of a personal life."

"What about Boden's groupies?" I interjected before I could stop myself.

Calvin gave me the slightest shake of his head, apparently signaling his displeasure at the interruption, but Tansy said promptly, "Oh, she didn't care about that. Picking up girls on the road isn't exactly the same thing as having a personal life. It wasn't as if he was seeing someone on a regular basis."

Before I could say anything else, Calvin returned to Doug. "So, Lilith discovered you were having an affair with her assistant, and you argued. What did she say?"

The other man's jaw hardened further, even as his gaze dropped to the cheerful blue patterned rug under his feet. "She told me she was firing me, that she wouldn't allow disloyalty on her team."

"Sounds like grounds for murder to me."

Those words made Doug Snyder propel himself up from the sofa. "Please," he said in disparaging tones. "I have a long list of other people just dying to work with me…so to speak. I didn't need Lilith Black. In fact, the whole setup of her traveling from place to place to perform her magic rituals was my idea."

Calvin looked over at Tansy. "Is this true?"

She nodded. "Yes."

"And did you know she was a complete fake?"

Dead quiet. I watched the girl's face, waiting to see the betrayal there…and not finding it.

"Yes."

So much for my judgment of human nature. I could have sworn that Tansy had bought into Lilith's act hook, line, and sinker. Apparently, she was a better actress than I thought.

Calvin didn't even blink. "Was she going to fire you, too?"

Tansy's teeth clamped down on her lower lip again. When she replied, though, she sounded resigned more than anything. "I think so. She hadn't said anything yet, but I could tell from the way she was acting that she was irritated with me, too. I think she was just waiting until this ritual was over and we were back in L.A. before she did anything about it. After all, if she fired me here, she would have had to manage all the packing up on her own."

That sounded like the Lilith Black we all knew and loved. Or at least, I had a feeling she'd make sure her own needs were looked after before she did anything so drastic as fire her faithful little shadow.

When neither Calvin nor I said anything, though, Tansy burst out, sounding much more impassioned this time, "We had nothing to do with Lilith's death! I don't know who killed her, but I know it wasn't either of us!"

From what Calvin had told me about the murder, I doubted that Tansy was responsible. She was too small and thin and frail. The angle of the knife would have been all wrong.

Doug, on the other hand....

"Don't leave town," Calvin said, and once again sent me the faintest of nods. This time, though, I understood that he was letting me know we were done here.

"So, what?" Doug demanded, voice angry now. "Are we under arrest?"

"Not at the moment," Calvin replied mildly.

"But this is an open investigation, and I might still have some questions. And if you think of anything you want to add, give me a call." He paused to pull a business card out of his pocket, then handed it to Doug before adding, "Thanks for your cooperation, and have a good day."

He nodded at the both of them before heading to the front door, with me at his heels. Once we were outside, I said, "You honestly think they're innocent?"

"I'm not sure 'innocent' is the right word," he said, then pointed the key fob at his SUV and unlocked the door. "But I also don't think they killed Lilith Black, even if they might have had a motive."

"So, what now?" I asked.

By that point we were both inside the vehicle and buckling our seat belts. His shoulders lifted, even as he touched a finger to the ignition button.

"Now?" he said, and paused. From the set of his mouth, I could tell he wasn't happy. "Now, we're back to square one."

14

Public Displays of Affection

For some reason, I'd never realized how frustrating police work could be. I suppose I'd naïvely thought that you followed an orderly set of clues and then ended up with a suspect. No muss, no fuss.

But although Calvin and I had learned a few interesting things during our interview with Doug Snyder and Tansy McCall, none of them seemed particularly actionable.

And then Calvin startled me by asking, "Buy you an early lunch?"

I sneaked a sideways glance at him. His focus was on the road, but I thought I detected something a bit too casual about the way his hands rested on the steering wheel. "Being seen in public with me?" I asked, trying not to sound too incredulous. "Isn't that kind of a big step?"

He didn't crack a smile. "Maybe. But I don't want to sneak around. If we're going to do this, then we need to be up front about it."

By "doing this," I assumed he meant try to have a normal relationship. And that meant going out to lunch.

"Oh, we're definitely doing this," I said firmly, even as I was doing a happy dance inside. "And lunch sounds great."

"Good. Is The Flatiron all right, or would you rather go to Olamendi's for Mexican?"

"The Flatiron is fine," I replied, even though I couldn't help but feel a slight stir of unease at the thought of eating there. After all, it was while I waited at that particular restaurant for Lucien to join me for a late breakfast that Calvin had showed up and taken me in for questioning regarding the GLANG leader's murder.

Speaking of which….

"What was with the hardline questioning yesterday morning?" I inquired. "You had me thinking you really did believe I murdered Lilith Black."

A smile finally made an appearance on his lips. Not a big one, but enough to show my question had had an impact. "Sorry about that," he said. "I guess it was rougher on me seeing you like that than I'd expected. You looked so tired and fragile. I just wanted to hold you and tell you everything was going to be okay, even though I knew I needed to stay impartial and that I couldn't do anything so personal. So I suppose I over-compensated."

"Yeah, just a little." Still, I couldn't be too angry with him. He'd known he needed to stay far away from me, and yet his first impulse had been to take me in his arms.

Just as I'd been longing to hold him at that exact same moment.

He let go of the steering wheel with his right hand and reached over so he could give my fingers a little squeeze. "I knew you couldn't have killed her. She'd given you plenty of reasons, but you're just not that kind of person."

Whereas I wasn't sure Lilith Black wouldn't have been capable of murder, if our roles had been reversed. I reflected it was probably a good thing that she hadn't actually practiced magic, because I could see her going down the left-hand path without too much hesitation.

"And that puts us right back to the problem of who actually did the deed," I said as Calvin pulled into the parking lot at The Flatiron. "And why."

Since at that point it was only a little after eleven, there weren't too many cars around. Generally, I didn't eat lunch before twelve-thirty or even one, but I'd only had a cup of Chobani and some fruit for breakfast, so I was ready for something more substantial.

"I know," Calvin replied. He put the SUV in park but didn't turn off the engine, instead leaving the motor running so we could have the benefit of the A/C. "And the problem is, although we interviewed as many of the attendees as we could, a lot of them weren't even staying in town. They drove here from the Phoenix area and disappeared as soon as the ritual was over. Tracking them down is going to be almost impossible."

"What about the tickets Lilith sold? Wouldn't you have credit card records or something?"

He shook his head. "She gave them away, same as you did. It made her look charitable, when she really makes most of her money from the monetization of her YouTube channel and endorsements on her Instagram account. There wasn't even a sign-in or anything like that where we could've at least collected email addresses or phone numbers."

That extra information did make our current situation seem even more dire. I was kind of surprised there was no type of accounting for who showed up, but I reminded myself that I hadn't provided any kind of check-in at my ritual, either. Not that I'd needed one, since all of my attendees had defected to go to Lilith's ceremony.

"Anyway," Calvin went on, "I did get her

laptop and phone from Tansy, along with her logins, so I have one of my guys taking a look at those now. I'm just hoping that if the killer was someone who actually knew her, there might be a clue hidden somewhere in her texts or in her social media accounts. Because if there isn't...."

The words trailed off, and the broad shoulders under their khaki uniform shirt seemed to hunch slightly. He didn't have to finish the sentence. If Lilith really had been murdered by a stranger attending the ritual—someone who had promptly disappeared to Phoenix or wherever—then we might never track him down.

That would be a definite black eye for the San Ramon Apache tribal police in general, and Calvin in particular. The murder of someone with as high a profile as Lilith Black didn't just go away overnight. People would be talking—and speculating—about the crime for quite a while, at least until the next sensation came along.

"Well," he said, his tone changing abruptly, "let's go in and get some food. I never had a chance to eat breakfast because I went into the station early today, and I'm running on coffee and not much else."

No arguments from me; I opened the door and got out, and Calvin shut off the engine and came to meet me so we could walk into the restaurant together. I noticed a few lifted eyebrows as we entered, but no one said anything, and we took a seat at a booth in the corner without over-hearing any murmurs.

He looked supremely unconcerned as he took a menu from the restaurant's owner, Ingrid, who was playing hostess that day, and ordered some iced tea. I asked for some as well, and we were left alone with our menus.

Since I'd gotten the hint that Calvin didn't want to discuss the case in public like this, I figured I might as well bring up a neutral topic of conversation. "Do you think we'll have an early or late monsoon this year?"

From the half-amused, half-pained expression that flitted across his face, I got the impression that he thought my change of subject was ham-handed at best. However, he played along, responding, "Hard to say. We've been dry for a couple of years, so some people think we're due for a change. I suppose we'll find out one way or another if we're patient."

Patience had never been one of my virtues, but I got his point. We could talk about the weather all we wanted, but that talking wouldn't change anything. "Well, I hope it's early. We hardly ever got any real thunderstorms in Southern California. Monsoon season sounds exciting."

"It can be…as long as your roof is in decent shape."

I couldn't help grinning. "It better be, since Ted Jenkins supposedly gave it a clean bill of health when I bought the place. I'd hate to have all my brand-new furniture ruined because of a crummy building inspector."

"Oh, if Ted looked it over, then you're in good shape." Calvin set down his menu as Ingrid approached, and ordered a grilled chicken sandwich with a side salad.

Because it was a hot day outside, I opted for chicken salad on a croissant, also accompanied by a side salad. Ingrid took our menus and said she'd have our food out in a bit, and disappeared into the kitchen.

Well, I'd exhausted the topic of the weather. I realized then there were so many things I wanted to talk about with Calvin—the investigation, the San Ramon tribe, the way Grandma Ellen had guided me to exactly the right spot the night before—but unfortunately, none of them were appropriate to a public conversation. And all right, we didn't have anyone seated in the booth directly behind us, and yet I knew I needed to be careful.

"So…." I said, then paused. Safe topics, safe topics…. "Did you go to school here in Globe?"

Another one of those knowing smiles curved

his mouth. I tried not to stare at it too hard, just because then I'd start thinking about how it felt when he kissed me, and I didn't want to get all hot and bothered in the middle of a restaurant in Globe at eleven in the morning.

"Not until high school," he replied. "We have our own K-8 school in San Ramon. But by the time we hit high school, we have kind of a handle on things, if you know what I mean."

I did, even though I had to wonder if a bunch of shape-shifting teenagers with rampaging hormones were actually that capable of keeping their coyote sides in check.

But I supposed the San Ramon tribal elders knew what they were doing. If nothing else, it was probably a good idea to have some integration with the community in Globe, even if the San Ramon Apache mostly kept to themselves.

Before I could say anything, though, Calvin went on. "And what about you?"

I shrugged. "Typical Southern California upbringing, I guess. I grew up in the Valley, mostly in Sherman Oaks."

"You don't sound like a Valley girl," he said, still smiling a little.

"Oh, I trained that out of myself." Which really wasn't that hard. I just made sure to sound like the people I saw reading the news or in my favorite TV shows...and honestly, the pure

"Valley girl" stereotype was just that—a stereotype. I'm not saying there weren't women in the San Fernando Valley who sounded like that, but they were in the minority. "Anyway, I went to Cal State Northridge for a couple of years and then dropped out. I knew an ordinary degree wasn't going to help me with what I really wanted to do with my life."

"Which was being a psychic."

He said it in a matter-of-fact way, with none of the condescension I was used to from most people. Then again, with his background, he also had to be open to the fact that there was a lot more in heaven and earth than your regular person on the street might believe.

"Yes," I replied. "I realized pretty early on that I had a gift. Luckily, my mother didn't try to keep me from using it."

"She's back in California?"

I nodded. "Yes. She got married about seven years ago." I didn't bother to add that the man she'd married was her former boss. There hadn't been any hanky-panky—he'd been divorced for years when they got together—but it still sounded kind of weird if you didn't know all the particulars. If things worked out between Calvin and me, then at some point I'd give him the whole story.

"And your father?"

This was starting to sound like another interrogation. I sipped some iced tea and said, "He's just a guy she hooked up with. They were never really together."

"So…he's not a part of your life?"

"Oh, we keep in touch," I replied. "He always paid child support and saw me around the holidays, that kind of thing. But my parents knew better than to try to get married because of me. He was a drummer in a band when they met."

Calvin took in that bit of information without blinking, for which I was grateful. A lot of the guys I'd dated—if they made it far enough to even learn anything about my family—tended to either look creepily knowing when I made that confession, or they seemed almost pitying, like it made sense that the illegitimate daughter of a drummer in a Valley-based hair band would decide to make her living as a psychic.

Ingrid showed up with our food then, and Calvin and I fell into a welcome silence as we started on our meals. It wasn't that I didn't like talking to him—the low, smooth sound of his voice was appealing enough without all the fabulousness of the total package—but I wished we could've been discussing the case. I might not have been a suspect anymore, and yet it was still something we needed to resolve.

A horrible thought struck me. What if the killing wasn't entirely personal? What if someone had just decided to start randomly killing witches? If that was really what was going on, maybe I was next.

No, that was silly. I'd slept in the clearing at Chuck's ranch all night by myself. Everyone knew where I was, so it would have been easy enough to slip over there and bury a knife in my back, or drop a garrote around my throat.

"You look worried," Calvin remarked, and I looked up from my chicken salad wrap to see him watching me, dark eyes thoughtful.

"Sorry," I said. "I guess I was manufacturing worst-case scenarios…like the killer might be after witches in general and not Lilith Black specifically."

He frowned, a faint worried line appearing in the smooth brown skin between his brows. "Damn. I hadn't thought of that."

"It's probably just me being paranoid."

"You don't seem like the paranoid type."

I actually wasn't, if only because the information I received from supernatural sources tended to prove that there was no such thing as conspiracy theories, only underlying patterns that were completely natural but which some people interpreted as sinister because they couldn't see the whole picture.

"I try not to be," I said lightly, and took a bite of my sandwich. After swallowing, I added, "I suppose I was just trying to make sense of all this. Doug Snyder and Tansy McCall had motive and opportunity, but that still doesn't feel right."

Calvin's face had gone still, and I knew he was worried that I was discussing sensitive information in a public place. Honestly, I hadn't meant to do that—I'd just been trying to work through the problem out loud, which tended to be a bad habit of mine.

"Sorry," I mumbled, and set down my sandwich so I could have a bite of salad.

"It's okay," he said. "I'm trying to figure it out, too. Right now, I think the best thing to do is wait and see if my team finds something on Lilith's laptop or phone."

It would be nice if they found a smoking gun, the one piece of evidence that would point directly back to the culprit. Unfortunately, I knew the world wasn't usually that neat.

However, since I also knew that Calvin really didn't want to keep discussing the case, I only nodded and went back to my lunch. Before too long, we were both done with our meal, and he was laying a couple of twenty-dollar bills down on the tabletop.

"I should be paying," I told him, feeling guilty. I had no idea how much he made as chief of the San Ramon tribal police, but I doubted it could compare to the inheritance I'd gotten from

Lucien Dumond, even if I'd been pretty dedicated to making sure large chunks of that money went to local charities.

"I asked you to lunch," he replied without hesitation. "Maybe sometime you can make me dinner again."

"Love to," I said. "How about tonight?"

The question got me a grin, which I'd hoped it would. "Maybe. Can't say for sure—I might be putting in some overtime today."

Right. He was working on an active murder investigation, even if he didn't want to be openly discussing it at the moment.

I couldn't help being a little disappointed, though. Still, I managed to smile and say, "Rain check?"

"Absolutely."

That settled, we got up from our table and headed out, saying a quick goodbye to Ingrid as we went.

"I'll need to drop you at home," Calvin said as I buckled my seat belt. "I know you want to help with the case, but if I bring you back to the station, people are going to wonder what's going on. You're a big help, but you're not an official part of the San Ramon tribal police."

"It's okay," I said quickly, even as I told myself that it really was. Calvin's and my relationship might have taken a quantum leap over the past twenty-four hours, but any help I gave him had to be by necessity strictly unofficial. Never mind any idle fantasies I might have had about becoming the tribal police's psychic for hire—the San Ramon people had very good reasons for keeping to themselves, and I knew I was already pushing it by becoming involved with one of their own.

Besides, the sign in the shop window at Once in a Blue Moon had said I would open at ten, and here it was almost noon. One could argue that a lot of the stores along Broad Street kept whimsical hours at best, but I didn't want to come off as a complete flake.

"I need to get back to work anyway," I added, and Calvin sent me a relieved smile.

"Right. I'll try to keep in touch as best I can."

I acknowledged that promise with a slight tilt of my head. Soon enough, we were pulling up to the back of my building. He turned off the engine, and I lifted an eyebrow.

"I figured I'd see you inside," he said. "Just in case there really are any serial witch killers on the loose."

From the glint in his eyes as he spoke, I guessed he really wasn't too worried about me getting ambushed by an axe murderer. No, I had a feeling I knew exactly what he wanted.

That hunch was borne out soon enough, because as soon as we were inside with the door safely closed behind us, he gave me another kiss, this one faintly flavored with honey mustard. Which was fine...I happened to love honey mustard.

It was a good, long kiss, one from which I emerged feeling slightly dizzy and not at all inclined to head into an afternoon of mundane work behind the counter at my shop. No, what I really wanted to do was drag him upstairs to my apartment and do unspeakable things to him. I'd just shoo Archie out into the hallway for the duration.

However, I knew that wasn't going to happen...mostly because Calvin pulled away immediately afterward, saying, "And now I really need to get going. With any luck, that kiss'll hold me for a bit."

"If not," I said with a grin, "I'd be all too happy to drive over to the police station and give you a booster to see you through the rest of the day."

"Don't tempt me." He touched my cheek, a caress that sent a delicious shiver through my body. "I'll try to call you if we come up with anything. You should be perfectly safe, but if you start to feel hinky about anyone coming into the shop, then just close up and give me a call."

His words put a slight damper on the afterglow from our kiss. What, was he having second thoughts about my serial killer theory?

All I said was, "Isn't this Chief Lewis's territory?"

"Technically. But if it's related to Lilith Black's murder, then it's my case."

I had to be satisfied with that. The Goddess only knew that I'd much rather deal with Calvin Standingbear than Globe's curmudgeon of a police chief. "Okay. But I'm sure everything will be fine."

Another kiss—this one hot enough to steam up my sunglasses—and Calvin was murmuring a goodbye and then disappearing out the door into the white-hot glare of the parking lot beyond. I stood for a moment in the dimly lit little foyer, smiling a bit foolishly at the memory of yet another unforgettable kiss.

Maybe it was wrong to be so happy when Lilith had died so horribly just two days earlier… but I just couldn't help myself.

15

Cooked Books

To say the rest of the afternoon was an anticlimax would be the understatement of the year. Because it was Thursday and I wouldn't have a real rush of customers until the weekend, the hours seemed to drag by. I got a new shipment of books and Tarot cards from Llewellyn Press, and so I used up a little time unpacking them and getting them properly entered into inventory before I put them out on the shelves, but it wasn't the sort of project that took up hours and hours.

However, Hazel came in a little after three, looking glowing and happy. She took one look at me and said, "You're all lit up. Are you absolved of Lilith Black's murder?"

"Yes," I replied, wondering if I should say anything about Calvin and me. Then again, he had told me he didn't want to sneak around.

Besides, if Hazel knew that Calvin and I had a thing going, then that should get rid of any lingering awkwardness about my one date with Chuck Langdon. "And Calvin and I worked everything out."

Her eyes widened. "You did? So...."

"So, we had lunch. And we'll be seeing each other again. I just don't know exactly when, since he's so busy right now with the murder investigation."

Usually, the mention of a murder was enough to dampen a person's enthusiasm, but Hazel still looked cheerful and rosy. "Oh, that's great news! Chuck and I went out to dinner last night, and it went really well. We're going to head over to Gilbert tomorrow to a place where he says we can go wine tasting."

Never in a million years would I have imagined Chuck Langdon as the type of guy who liked to go wine tasting, but people did have a tendency to surprise you. Or maybe he'd suggested the activity because he knew it was the sort of thing Hazel would enjoy.

"I'm so glad for you two," I said, and I meant it. Chuck and Hazel were both extremely nice people, and they deserved to be happy. "You'll have to report back on the wine tasting. It sounds like something Calvin and I might want to try when he isn't so busy."

"I will. There are also a lot of places in Scottsdale for that kind of thing, but we'll probably wait for the fall when it isn't so hot."

Was Gilbert appreciably cooler than Scottsdale? I had no idea, since I was only slowly coming to any kind of knowledge about the greater Phoenix area. Maybe Gilbert simply seemed more doable because it was so much closer.

"Anyway," she went on, "I just wanted to check in because I was worried about you. The last time we talked, things didn't seem to be going so well. I'm glad that you and Calvin patched things up, and that no one thinks you could have had anything to do with Lilith's murder."

That might have been taking things a bit too far—after all, I hadn't done a poll of Globe's residents to see what they thought of the situation—but I supposed just the visual of me going about my business, clearly a free woman, had probably done a lot to dispel anyone's suspicions.

"I hope so," I said lightly, figuring I might as well leave it there. "Maybe sometime after this investigation is behind him, Calvin and I can get together with you and Chuck to do dinner or something."

As I spoke, though, I hoped I wasn't getting ahead of myself. Maybe Calvin wasn't a double-date kind of guy.

Hazel nodded, looking pleased. "Oh, that would be fun. Let me know."

"I will."

She left soon after that, and I tried to keep myself busy by reorganizing some of the books that had gotten out of alphabetical order, and then wandering around the shop with a feather duster. The place was already pretty much dust-free, but at least it looked as if I was doing something.

I made myself stick it out until five, mostly because I'd come in late and it would have looked extra-bad to close early on top of that. It was with a sigh of relief that I locked the front doors, turned off the lights, and headed upstairs to my apartment. As I went, I got out my phone and checked it for any missed calls or messages.

Not a damn thing.

Well, Calvin had told me that he'd get in touch when he could. I had to believe the investigation must have consumed his entire day.

Archie was nowhere in evidence when I entered the apartment. Well, since I'd had lunch so early, his own midday meal had only been delayed by ten minutes or so, and therefore he didn't have much reason to be irritated with me… especially since I was home from work right on time and he didn't have to worry about dinner.

A quick peek told me the cat was sleeping in

his bed in the office. I grabbed my laptop from the desk and headed back out to the living room, figuring I might as well start looking up some fun new recipes for whenever it would be okay to have Calvin over for dinner. As I surfed around on Pinterest, however, I realized I'd never told him anything about Archie. I'd need to broach that subject at some point, if only to let him know our meals—and anything else—wouldn't be quite as private as he imagined.

Maybe I should offer to cook Calvin a meal at his house. That seemed safer…and besides, I was jonesing to try out that gorgeous Viking six-burner stove of his.

I also realized we hadn't seen hide nor hair of Boden Marsh when we went over to the Airbnb where supposedly all of them had been staying. He couldn't have left town already, could he?

No, Calvin had told everyone in Lilith's group they needed to stay put during this initial phase of the investigation. More likely, Boden had decided to make himself scarce as soon as he heard Doug Snyder was coming over. I had to believe that if Lilith knew about Tansy and Doug's affair, then Boden probably did, too. He seemed like exactly the sort of guy who would want to remove himself from an awkward situation and stay far, far away.

On an impulse, I closed my laptop and set it on the coffee table, then pulled my phone out of the skirt pocket where I'd stowed it. No missed calls or messages, but that wasn't why I wanted to look at it.

Instead, I opened Instagram and checked my most recent post, the one about my preparation for the ritual. It had gotten a handful of likes, including a couple of forlorn comments from people who said it sounded like fun and they wished they could come, but it was way too far to travel.

I tried not to sigh. It seemed as though the people who were actual fans were the only ones who hadn't come to Globe at all.

The other thing I noticed was that my follower count had dropped precipitously, from a high of almost two hundred thousand to only a little more than six thousand. Had word about the debacle spread so quickly that everyone had dropped me like the proverbial hot potato?

It sure seemed that way...and I really couldn't find it within me to care. After all, I'd already decided to delete the whole thing anyway. This experience had told me social media and I definitely weren't a good combination. Whether my prosperity spell had backfired or whether Lilith and Tansy had been meddling behind the scenes, I couldn't say for sure, although both prospects sounded equally plausible. All I knew for certain was that I'd be all too happy to say goodbye to Instagram after this was all over.

In the meantime, since I had the app open, I thought I might as well check out Lilith's feed. There was a tearstained video posted by Tansy, telling everyone in her breathy little voice what had happened and how they were now trying to figure out what to do with Lilith's account.

"She taught me so much about the craft," Tansy said near the end, eyes big and tragic, ringed with runny mascara. "And I want to consecrate her memory by continuing her work. I don't want to take over her account, but you can follow me over at @Tansy underscore Flower underscore Magic to see how I carry on with Lilith Black's work."

Interesting. I looked up her account; it already had more than a hundred and fifty thousand followers.

Maybe they were all the people who'd ditched me.

I couldn't even be annoyed. If Tansy wanted to ride Lilith's coattails, more power to her. Who knows—maybe she was even a real witch, unlike her former boss.

"What was that noise?" Archie said in an irritated tone as he came around a corner of the sofa. "Are you watching soap operas again?"

"I don't watch soap operas," I retorted,

246 • CHRISTINE POPE

sounding nearly as annoyed as the cat. "If you're referring to Hallmark Channel movies, that's something *entirely* different."

Generally, I wouldn't touch the Hallmark Channel with a ten-foot pole. However, I'd gotten a little maudlin as Calvin's radio silence had continued over the past few months, and drowning myself in a bunch of silly happily-ever-afters—and a judicious amount of rocky road ice cream—had seemed like the safest remedy.

"Someone was crying," the cat remarked in accusing tones, making it sound as if experiencing a human emotion was the height of weakness. Maybe to Archie, it was. I didn't know if it was all the years trapped in cat form or whether he really had been that cold-hearted when he was a man, but he did seem like the most unempathetic human being I'd ever met. That witch might have actually done him a favor by changing him into a creature more closely aligned with his natural temperament.

"It was an Instagram post by Lilith Black's assistant," I said, waving my phone at the cat, although I had a feeling he couldn't have cared less. "She's a little upset right now."

He sniffed. "I don't see why. She seemed like a thoroughly unpleasant person."

"Who was brutally murdered."

A flick of his tail, and Archie wandered off

into the kitchen so he could lap some water from the bowl placed on the floor there. Once he was done, he came back out into the living room, and said, "Don't tell me *you're* upset she's dead."

Well, I couldn't tell him that, because it wouldn't have been the truth. Or rather, I didn't think anyone deserved such a brutal fate, and I was genuinely sorry that Lilith's last moments on this earth had been ones of pain. But I certainly wasn't going to lie and say I was heartbroken over the whole thing.

"No," I said, and I could have sworn the glance Archie slanted at me then was almost approving, as if he'd expected me to make some sort of halfhearted politically correct protest and was pleasantly surprised that I'd admitted I didn't really care one way or the other. "But that doesn't mean I don't want to find out what happened to her. I mean, I did this whole Instagram thing to attract tourists to Globe, and the only thing that happened was we ended up with another murder here. Like that's going to be any kind of enticement to visit."

Archie jumped up onto the armchair and settled himself in the exact center of the cushion. Golden eyes fixed on me, he remarked, "I wouldn't be so sure about that. Humans seem to be attracted to be scenes of violence. Some kind of perverse curiosity, I suppose."

I opened my mouth to contradict him and then realized he was partially right. There had been tours of famous crime scenes back in L.A., after all. And I knew people scooped up books on serial killers by the millions. Also, when you got right down to it, many ghost tours also happened to be tours of crime scenes, just because a lot of spirits lingered in the places where they'd met a violent end.

After a pause, I said, "Maybe, but I don't think that's what Josie had in mind when she encouraged me to get on social media and make Globe a happening place."

"Probably not."

I closed the Instagram app and set the phone down on the coffee table next to my laptop. Looking at it reminded me of why I'd gotten out my computer in the first place. Should I mention to Archie that I'd started seeing Calvin Standingbear again, just to warn him that I might be having an overnight guest in the near future?

Maybe that would have been wise, but Archie was being remarkably mellow—for him—and I didn't feel like rocking the boat. Besides, I'd already gotten myself set on the idea of cooking for Calvin at his house. I might have been using his gorgeous kitchen as an easy excuse, but I knew a big part of it was that I also didn't want to deal with the concept of having sex while a cat that used to be a man was sleeping just down the hall.

Of course, I was probably jumping the gun. Our kisses told me Calvin and I had some serious chemistry, but it would probably be a good idea to have at least a couple of proper dates before we took that kind of step.

I just hoped I could hold out that long. Every time our eyes met, it felt like someone throwing a lit match on gasoline-soaked rags.

My phone gave a single clear chime just then, telling me I had a new text message. I grabbed for it and checked the home screen.

Calvin.

Still working, the text said. *It's going to be a late one. We found an email dated a few days ago from Lilith's accountant, wanting to go over some discrepancies in her business account, but she never replied. It came in right before the ritual, so maybe she read it and thought she'd answer the next day when she had more time.*

A day that had never come for her. I couldn't help experiencing a twinge of sadness at that thought, just because I knew it was such a common thing for us mortals—we put things off, always thinking we had more time.

However, I pushed the melancholy away and reread the message. Discrepancies in her business account? That could have meant almost anything.

But maybe the accountant had wanted to phrase the email in a neutral way, since he—or she—didn't have all the facts yet.

Who would have access to Lilith's accounts?

Doug Snyder, probably. He was her business manager, after all, and there was definitely something about the guy that rubbed me the wrong way. However, I had to admit that an instinctual dislike of a person didn't necessarily equate to actual guilt, even though my gut feelings about people tended to be fairly accurate.

And Tansy? That was harder to say. She was Lilith's assistant, but had Lilith trusted her enough to give her access to her bank accounts?

I had no idea…and because Calvin had pretty much told me to stay out of it for now while he worked, I couldn't exactly pick up my phone and shoot Tansy a DM at the Instagram account she'd mentioned in her teary video.

That sort of restriction would have put a lot of people back to square one. However, I had resources that most people didn't.

Archie appeared to have slipped off into one of his innumerable naps while I was reading Calvin's text. I got up from the sofa and tiptoed into the office, then shut the door behind me. It wasn't so much that I cared whether the cat knew what I was up to, and more that I simply didn't want to be interrupted.

A brief glance at the box that held my two favorite sets of Tarot cards, and then I shook my head. Maybe the cards would be able to provide a few useful clues, but I had something far more important in mind.

I took hold of my office chair and rolled it across the room to plant it in front of the table that held my altar. After sitting down, I placed my hands on the crystal ball and said, "Grandma Ellen, I need to speak with you."

No response. Well, sometimes she was busy, off doing whatever it was that filled her endless afterlife days. Part of the reason why I'd gotten the chair was that I planned to keep my rear end planted in the seat until I got a response.

"Grandma Ellen, this is urgent."

A faint mist swirled inside the crystal ball. It felt almost icy to the touch, although I had to admit that could simply have been because it had been sitting in the direct flow from the air conditioning vent above the table before I moved the crystal ball closer to me.

The mist grew more solid, resolved itself into the form of my grandmother's head. She didn't always take shape in such a way, but when she did, I got the impression it was in fact because she'd been off occupied with something else when I called out to her.

Her blue eyes opened, gazing into mine.

"What is it, Selena? Didn't my advice work out for you last time?"

I blinked, then realized she was talking about me finding the answers to my questions if I went to the location where Lilith Black had been murdered. "No, it worked out fine. I learned the truth about Calvin, and we worked things out."

My grandmother smiled. "Good. He seems like a nice boy. So handsome!"

I allowed myself an inward smile at the incongruity of my grandmother—whose spirit looked barely forty—calling someone who was only five or six years younger a "boy."

Especially since the "boy" in question was a solid six feet, four inches of muscular hotness.

"Yes, he is," I agreed, and left it at that. "But there was something else I needed to know—who killed Lilith Black?"

At once, her mouth tightened ever so slightly. "I can't tell you that."

Can't, or won't? I thought, although I didn't ask the question out loud. In the spirit world, those were often the same things. My fingers tightened on the crystal ball as I asked, "Why not?"

Her expression softened. "My dear, I am here to be your guide, but I can't do everything for you. What I can say is that you already know everything you need to know. All you have to do now is put the pieces together."

Easy for her to say. She'd been observing all these events as a dispassionate onlooker, while I was embroiled in the thick of things. My first instinct was to pin the crime on Doug Snyder, but I also had to remind myself that just because I disliked the guy for getting involved with someone way too young and inexperienced for him, it didn't mean he was a killer.

"Not even a teeny little hint?" I asked, and Grandma Ellen smiled.

"Not even that. My dear, you are a very strong psychic. It's just that sometimes, you get in your own way. I've seen that you're no longer under suspicion, so there's no reason to have desperation drive you. Let yourself be open to the knowledge you already possess."

I wanted to snap that her advice sounded like the typical woo-woo counsel any cut-rate psychic would offer when she didn't actually have any true insights to give. However, that would be incredibly rude—and probably wrong as well. Just because I didn't like what she was saying didn't mean her words weren't valid.

Holding in a sigh, I said, "I'll do my best."

A smile still curved her lips as she replied, "That's all anyone can expect from themselves. Trust in the process, Selena. You can do this."

After delivering those words, she faded from view. I still clutched the crystal ball, but I knew if I tried to summon her again, she wouldn't respond.

It looked like I'd have to do this on my own.

16

Pillow Talk

WELL, FIRST THINGS FIRST. I WASN'T FEELING particularly insightful or clever, and so I figured the best thing for me to do until inspiration struck was to make myself some herbal tea and take a breath, then assess.

Archie was still asleep on his chair in the living room when I emerged from the office. I took a brief detour to pick up my phone from the coffee table and see if I'd missed any messages or texts, but my phone remained stubbornly silent.

Right then, I really wished I could be with Calvin as he and his team pored over the contents of Lilith's laptop and phone. Maybe one of those items contained a piece of evidence that wouldn't make any sense to the tribal police but would immediately jump out at me.

Or maybe you won't be able to see anything, either, I scolded myself as I headed into the kitchen, then filled the kettle with water and set it to boil. *It's not like you're some great forensic data analyst or something.*

True enough. But my grandmother seemed to think I had all the necessary facts at my disposal, even if right then I couldn't figure out what they could possibly be.

Frowning, I got a mug out of the cupboard and then found some of my favorite herbal tea, the fragrant one with rose hips and lemon and a hint of vanilla. As edgy as I was feeling, I knew that having any more caffeine after the iced tea I'd drunk at lunch probably wasn't a good idea.

I watched my cheerful blue kettle and pondered the problem. The manner of Lilith's killing seemed to suggest it had been a spur-of-the-moment sort of thing, and not the kind of crime that had been premeditated in any way. Someone had been pushed over the edge, and had lashed out.

Which seemed to tell me it had to have been someone who knew her. I suppose if one of her diehard fans had found out she was a complete charlatan, the revelation might have been enough to send someone into a murderous rage...but that explanation somehow didn't feel right to me.

Besides, if one of those anonymous attendees at her ritual really was guilty, I knew we'd have a heck of a time trying to discover who they were.

Better to stick with a much smaller—and more plausible—pool of suspects.

I'd been dismissive of Tansy, but maybe I should reexamine the possibility that she was guilty. People could manage all sorts of crazy feats of strength when pushed to the limit. Yes, the angle of attack seemed wrong, but maybe she'd jumped off a tree stump or something.

Despite the seriousness of the situation, I couldn't help grinning at the thought of Tansy launching herself at Lilith from a stump like some sort of rabid flying squirrel. The theory did seem a little crazy.

All right, then Doug Snyder. He was certainly big enough to have overpowered Lilith. No, he wasn't as muscular as Calvin, who looked like he might chop a cord of wood for fun—and for all I knew, maybe he did. There was certainly enough firewood piled up on the side of his house for that notion to be entirely plausible.

But even though Doug didn't exactly have the appearance of a man who chopped down trees in his spare time, he seemed fit enough, like someone who put in an hour at the gym every day not because he enjoyed it, but because he wanted to present a certain physical image to his clients. And he was definitely enough taller than Lilith that he could have sunk a knife into her back at the proper angle without any problem. He'd said he didn't care that she was planning to fire him, but those words could have been merely bravado. After all, he definitely didn't seem like the sort of man who would want to admit any kind of defeat. Maybe it was true that he had lots of other clients on the line…and maybe it wasn't. Even so, having someone like Lilith Black fire you wasn't going to look too great on a resume.

Especially if she just happened to mention that fact to her two million Instagram followers.

Then my thoughts slid around to Boden Marsh. I told myself I had to consider him a suspect, even if I didn't want to. For all I knew, he'd put forth the pretense of being friendly and open and not at all threatening just so I would dismiss his possible guilt out of hand. I hadn't gotten any bad vibes off him, but, to be fair, I hadn't sensed that Violet Clarke had been an accessory to Lucien Dumond's murder, either. Sometimes those sorts of things managed to slip past you, no matter how attuned you thought your psychic senses might be.

The teakettle began to emit a faint whistle, and I turned off the gas before the water could start to truly boil. After pouring water over the waiting teabag in the mug I'd set out, I took the cup with me to the living room. Archie was gone, and since I hadn't been paying him much attention, I didn't know where he'd slipped off. Probably back to his favorite spot in the office, but I wouldn't bother to go check.

I stood for a moment next to the couch, realizing that Boden had sat there just a few days earlier. Had I been playing hostess to a murderer without knowing it?

Possibly.

A shiver went down my spine that had nothing to do with the air conditioning blasting away in the background. The mug was almost uncomfortably warm against my cold hands, and I went ahead and set it down on a coaster. I needed to let the tea steep for a few minutes before I could drink it, anyway.

Thus unencumbered, I stood for a moment, staring at the couch and thinking of the man who'd sat there only two days earlier.

Was Boden Marsh really capable of killing Lilith Black?

My grandmother's words echoed in my mind.

You already know everything you need to know.

I wanted to complain that it was easy enough for her to say. Then again, she had the proper perspective, and I didn't. The view from the afterlife was much broader than anything we could see with our mortal eyes.

If I already knew something, how could I let myself know that I knew it?

I ran a hand through my hair and pushed with annoyed fingers at my bangs, trying to get them to lie flat and behave. For several weeks, I'd been planning to get a trim, but something had always seemed to come up and get in the way.

One of the throw pillows on the couch looked slightly squashed. Was that where Boden had leaned back during our conversation? I supposed it was possible; I'd been too busy the past few days to lounge on the sofa, and besides, I usually sat at the other end so I'd have a better view of the screen when I was watching TV.

On a sudden impulse, I stepped forward and grabbed the pillow. I'd never done much with my powers of psychometry—the talent for getting psychic flashes from touching inanimate objects—but I knew I had them, even if they weren't as developed as some of my other skills.

Fingers clenched on the nubby linen fabric, I thought, *Let me see Boden.*

Nothing. Right then, I was really glad no one was around to see me standing in the middle of my living room, holding on to a pillow for dear life.

However, I resisted the impulse to toss it onto

the couch in disgust. No, I continued to hang on to the thing, willing it to give up its secrets, to let me see what was happening with the man who'd leaned against it only forty-eight hours earlier.

The briefest flash of an image swirled in my mind—Boden sitting with a pretty girl who looked like she was in her early twenties, with long fawn-brown hair and a heart-shaped face with high cheekbones. They sat on a couch, feet up on the coffee table in front of them. All the furniture in the room looked almost brand-new, as if it had been recently ordered out of a catalogue or something.

That was all I got before the image faded. Still, it told me that Boden wasn't alone, that obviously he'd found someone to take him in while he made himself scarce.

I thought then of the girl he'd mentioned to me, the one he'd hooked up with after Lilith's ritual.

What was her name?

It took me a minute to rifle through all the memories of the past few crazy days, but then it popped into my brain.

Emily.

No last name, although that didn't necessarily have to be a huge problem. After all, I was pretty good friends with a woman who had an encyclopedic knowledge of everyone in Globe.

I sat down on the couch—at the opposite end from where Boden had sat—and picked up my mug of tea and took a very cautious sip. It was still too hot, and I thought I just barely escaped burning my tongue.

That little sip was all I needed, though. I put down the mug and reached for my phone, then went through my contacts until I got to Josie Woodrow's entry. As I touched the green button to call her, I prayed she wasn't showing a house or doing something else that might prevent her from answering.

To my relief, she picked up on the second ring. "Selena!" she exclaimed. "How are you? I heard that Calvin questioned you, but then Hazel said—"

"I'm fine," I cut in, but gently. It was heart-warming to know she'd been worried about me. "Everything's okay. I wanted to ask you something, though."

"Go ahead."

In the background, I thought I heard voices murmuring, and I said, "I'm not interrupting anything, am I?"

"Oh, I'm showing a house, but it's their second viewing, so they don't really need me for anything. They just wanted to do a second walk-through so they could make sure their furniture would fit."

Josie sounded breezy and unconcerned, although I couldn't help feeling guilty for the way I'd called while she was working. Still, I thought I might as well let it go. She knew what she was doing.

"Okay," I replied. "I was just wondering if you knew anyone in town named Emily. She'd be in her early twenties, with long, light brown hair. Pretty."

"That sounds like Emily Porter," Josie said at once, although something in her voice sounded faintly disapproving. "She inherited quite a bit of money from one of her great-aunts, and bought a house from me about a year ago. I have a feeling if she doesn't watch what she's doing, she'll be out of cash before she's twenty-five…but I'm sure that's none of my business."

Since I was alone, I allowed myself a smile. Josie always did have a way of telling you a variety of intimate details about various people in the town, generally followed by the disclaimer that it wasn't any of her business.

"Where's Emily's house?" I asked, and even though I couldn't see her, I got the impression that Josie's expression had suddenly sharpened.

"Why?"

"I, um…." I fumbled for a plausible explanation as to why I'd go seeking out a girl I didn't even know, then said hastily, "She came in the store and bought a pair of earrings, but she left the package behind. Since she paid cash, I didn't know who she was or where she lived. That's why I thought I'd ask you."

"Oh, that does sound like Emily. She always was something of a scatter-brain. Well, her house is on Bailey Street, near the top of the hill. Number thirty-two."

"Thanks, Josie," I said, excitement prickling through me. Maybe this would be an utter dead end, but I had to try. If nothing else, I might learn a little more about Boden Marsh from someone outside Lilith Black's orbit.

"It's nothing," Josie replied. "Although I do think it's going above and beyond for you to stop by her house. Do you want her number? You could call and have her come down to the shop."

"No, that's fine," I returned hastily. "I've been cooped up in here all day—it'll be good to get out for a little bit."

"Cooped up after your lunch with Calvin Standingbear, you mean."

It truly amazed me how Josie seemed to have spies everywhere. There hadn't even been that many people eating at The Flatiron when Calvin and I had shown up, and yet the news had certainly gotten to her fast enough.

Ingrid being chatty, most likely.

"Yes," I said, doing my best to sound casual,

even though I guessed it was a lost cause. "We had lunch."

"And?"

"And...I think it's going to be okay," I told her, which seemed safe enough. After all, Calvin and I had already determined that we wanted to make a go of things. I just wouldn't provide Josie with any real details.

"Oh, that's wonderful!" A pause while a man's voice said something indistinct, and then Josie added, "I have to run. But I hope you can catch Emily at home."

So do I, I thought, even as I said a quick goodbye and ended the call.

And also, thank the Goddess—and all the other gods and goddesses of the various pantheons —for Josie Woodrow. Sometimes the town busybody was exactly what you needed.

I almost grabbed my purse and ran out the door there and then, but I knew I needed to put some food in Archie's bowl, just in case this took longer than I thought and I ended up staying away until well after the cat's six-thirty suppertime. So I got a can of cat food out of the pantry, opened it, and dumped the gooey, fish-smelling mass into his bowl, then called out, "Archie! I fed you!"

No response for a moment, and then he wandered into the dining room and sent a baleful glance toward me. "It's only five forty-five."

"I know," I said, trying to sound patient. "But I'm going out and don't know when I'll be back. I wanted to make sure you were taken care of."

That was generally the point where someone would have said "thank you." Since it was Archie, he only gave a dismissive sniff and headed back down the hall.

I told myself to count to five…or maybe fifteen.

No, I didn't have that kind of time. It was still early for most people to be thinking of eating dinner, but I couldn't dismiss the possibility that Emily might decide to head out somewhere to get some takeout or whatever.

Instead, I sent a quick message to Calvin, telling him I wanted to go talk to Emily Porter, since I thought she might be connected to Boden Marsh. I'd hesitated before doing so, but then decided it was better to face his wrath for meddling in the investigation than to walk blind into a situation without any backup. At least this way, he'd know where I'd gone.

That matter handled, I went downstairs and got into my car. The portable carport Brett Woodrow put up for me had reduced some of the intense heat that had been baking into the car all day, but I still felt as though I was gasping for air as I turned on the A/C full blast and cracked the windows to let out some of the accumulated heat. Since I wasn't going far, I wondered if the car would even have a chance to cool down before I reached my destination.

The street where Emily Porter's house was located turned out to be one of the steepest in hilly Globe, and so I was glad that I'd decided to drive, even though it was less than half a mile away. Her place was a little bigger than most on the street, a sturdy farmhouse-style place painted cream with dark red shutters. It seemed large for someone who supposedly lived by herself, but I guessed that maybe she'd wanted to make a splash with her inheritance.

A new-looking Mustang convertible was parked in the driveway, shimmering red in the sun. Yes, it was almost six, but at that time of year, the sun didn't seem too inclined to sink behind the horizon any time soon.

I took the coward's way out and parked half a block away, with my dusty blue Beetle halfway hidden behind a neighbor's big Chevy truck. For some reason, it just felt safer to not be too obvious about my approach.

Of course, once I reached Emily Porter's property, I couldn't do much to hide myself. Rosebushes marched their way along on either side of the patterned brick front walk, but they certainly weren't tall enough to conceal an adult person.

Well, I just had to hope that she wasn't sitting in any of the front rooms, staring out the window to see who might be dropping by for a visit.

As I went up the front walk, a little shiver walked its way down my spine. Suddenly, this didn't seem like such a good idea.

Don't be a baby, I scolded myself. *You're the one who wanted to get to the bottom of Lilith's murder, and Emily Porter has some kind of connection with Boden Marsh. Ring the darn doorbell and act like a grown-up.*

With those bracing inner admonitions to guide me, I reached out and touched the button mounted next to the front door. It rang with a no-nonsense *ding-dong.*

I waited, resisting the impulse to reach up and smooth my hair. No, what I really needed to do was rehearse what I planned to say to Emily Porter so I wouldn't sound like a lunatic.

Hi, Emily. I heard you hooked up with Boden Marsh the night of Lilith Black's ritual. Did you know there's a strong possibility he might be her killer? Did he say anything to you before, during, or after you had sex?

Right.

So sorry to bother you, Emily, but I got a psychic flash that you were hanging out with

Boden Marsh, and I just wanted to let you know he could be a murderer.

I didn't get any further than that, because the door opened, and Boden gazed down at me, a curiously resigned expression on his face.

"I thought you might find me here," he said.

17

Bonnie and Clyde

BEFORE I COULD RESPOND—MOSTLY BECAUSE my mouth was waggling, and I didn't know whether to come up with some kind of cogent answer or just turn tail and run—he reached out and grabbed me by the arm, and hauled me inside.

"Ow," I said indignantly, once I'd recovered myself. "What the hell do you think you're doing?"

"Getting you inside where no one can see you," he replied, which didn't do much to soothe my nerves. "How did you do it?"

I didn't bother to ask what he meant by "it." I pointed at my head, and he released a sigh.

"Just what I thought." He gestured toward the space off to our left, which looked like the living room. "Go sit down."

"Is Emily here?" I asked, staying firmly planted in the foyer, my feet practically glued to the ceramic planks underneath. From what I could see of the house, it looked thoroughly updated, but also oddly soulless, as if whoever had decorated it had taken every idea directly from a show on HGTV without putting anything of their own personality into the place. "I need to talk to her."

"She's busy," Boden said.

However, his eyes wouldn't meet mine, and I caught sluggish red pulses emanating from his aura.

Guilt...and something worse.

"What did you do?" I demanded, worry surging through me.

"She kept asking questions," Boden said. "So...I made her stop."

I swallowed. He still seemed completely calm, almost easygoing, and yet underneath it all, I sensed the horror of the crimes he'd committed over the past several days.

For the moment, I figured it was better to go along with what he wanted. I hadn't sensed any hostility toward me...yet...but I guessed his emotions could turn on a dime.

I went into the living room and sat down on the slipcovered sofa there. "Why Emily, Boden?" I asked.

There was a half-drunk bottle of Steiner Bock sitting on the coffee table, the sweaty container leaving a ring on the polished surface. He picked it up and took a swallow, then said, "I didn't want to, but after Doug Snyder came around—"

"You talked to Doug?" I cut in. "When?"

"Earlier this afternoon. He told me that he'd been in touch with Lilith's accountant and wanted to hear my side of things." Boden drank some more beer before adding, "I told him I didn't have anything to say, but he started shouting at me, yelling all sorts of accusations. Emily heard the whole thing, and after he was gone, she started asking way too many questions."

"Where is she, Boden?" I asked, a trickle of nervous sweat sliding down my back. The house had air conditioning, as far as I could tell, but it still felt uncomfortably warm in here.

"Upstairs." He paused and set down the bottle, dark eyes piercing as he stared at me. "You understand why I did it, don't you?"

"Did what?" I asked, trying to play dumb.

Boden tilted his head, thin mouth quirking in a lopsided smile. Maybe he'd hoped his expression would look guileless—or at least endearing—but he really only looked crazy.

Which was entirely the problem.

"Oh, I think you know what," he said. His thumbs hooked around the loops of his faded jeans, and he rocked back slightly on the heels of his scuffed motorcycle boots. "But I really didn't have any choice."

Somehow, I managed to swallow, even though my throat felt as dry as the rocky hillsides that surrounded the town. "We always have a choice, Boden."

I wasn't sure why, but that comment seemed to amuse him. His smile broadened, making him look positively shark-like, and he said, "Maybe. But there wasn't really anything else I could have done." Suddenly, his expression sobered, and he reached over and took me by the wrist. Those thin fingers felt a lot stronger than they looked, and again a shiver made its way down my spine as I thought of how he'd thrust that knife straight into Lilith's back.

"Let me go, Boden," I told him, trying my best to keep the words calm, even. I couldn't afford to freak out right then, not when I knew he was walking a knife edge when it came to maintaining control.

"What if I don't want to?" He pulled me closer, and he stared down into my face, even as something softened about the set of his mouth.

However, I didn't find that shift at all reassuring. Just the opposite, actually.

When I didn't respond, he went on, "You and I would make a great team, you know. Your powers are real. Just think what kind of a following you could get."

"Oh, like all the people who said they'd come to my ritual and then ghosted me?"

Boden shook his head. "Only because Lilith interfered. But she won't be a problem anymore."

And, thanks to Chuck, I knew exactly how she'd interfered—with an Instagram story saying how her ritual would be much better and that people shouldn't attend mine. I'd been busy and hadn't been following her posts as closely as I probably should, and I completely missed the story, an oversight made even easier by the way Instagram stories disappeared after twenty-four hours anyway.

I made myself stand completely still. Boden was way too close for comfort, but I had the feeling that any movement I made, he'd be on me in a second. As it was, he was maintaining his distance...for the moment.

"Maybe," I lied, hating myself for the spark of hope that flickered in his eyes after I made that answer...and also knowing the best thing I could do was stall for time. Just where the hell was Calvin, anyway? I'd sent him that text almost twenty minutes earlier.

But Calvin could have been hip-deep in something at the station, and maybe wasn't checking his phone as often as he should. I had to believe he'd look eventually…just as I also hoped and prayed I could keep Boden going long enough for the cavalry to show up.

"You need to tell me the truth, though," I added. "If you want me to work with you, I have to know what happened."

Something flickered in his eyes, and he hesitated for a moment, even as I noted another series of red pulses before his aura faded again. "You'll be angry," he said.

"No, I won't," I told him. Although I generally tried to be truthful with everyone, I thought this was one instance where a few lies were warranted. "What makes me angry is when people try to hide the truth from me."

Another pause. "Okay." He smiled then, expression suddenly shifting into something sunny, a look that felt so off-kilter, I had to keep myself from tearing my wrist from his grasp and bolting for the door.

How had he been able to hide his madness from Lilith and everyone around him?

Unfortunately, as I'd told Calvin just a few days earlier, people tended to believe what they wanted to believe. Lilith had probably overlooked the warning signs because she liked having such an obedient slave. And honestly, wasn't I guilty of the same thing? I'd also tried to convince myself that Boden couldn't possibly be the murderer because he seemed like such a nice guy.

"I was skimming some money out of her business account," he said, looking singularly unconcerned by this confession of his casual embezzling. "I knew she would never notice, because she thought paying attention to that sort of thing was beneath her. And it wasn't a lot—a couple thousand bucks a month at the most."

Well, that was a lot of money to a lot of people. There were quite a few residents of Globe who got by on that much each month, if not even less. However, since I guessed Boden wouldn't much care for me pointing out that little fact, I kept my mouth shut.

He ran a distracted hand through his shaggy hair, even while he maintained his death grip on my wrist with his other hand. "But I guess her accountant noticed. Lilith confronted me the night of the ritual, told me there was going to be a reckoning when we got back to L.A. I tried to laugh it off, but she said Doug had evidence, and that she'd make sure I went to jail." He stopped there, mouth hardening. "I couldn't let that happen, not with my priors."

"Priors?" I asked, the word coming out as a pitiful little squeak. So much for maintaining my cool.

A careless shrug. "Possession…one count of assault. Nothing major."

I didn't exactly view assault as a minor crime, but I thought it was probably better to refrain from comment. "So, you picked up Lilith's athame and stabbed her with it."

The humorless, shark-like smile returned. "I figured that was a fitting end for her. She used the knife as a prop, so I thought I'd show her it actually had its uses. Of course, she wasn't expecting me to come back after everyone else had gone. That was a fun little surprise for her."

Once again, I tried to swallow against the dryness in my throat. "And then you left the crime scene."

"Yes. I wiped the hilt and headed over here." He glanced upward, as if to the room where poor Emily's body must be lying even as we spoke.

I tried not to shudder. "Didn't Emily ask where you'd gone?"

Boden shrugged. "I told her I'd left something at the ritual site and needed to go back to get it."

"So…she lied to the police when she told them you were with her all night?"

"Yeah. She honestly wasn't a fan of Lilith. She told me she'd only gone to the ritual because she was bored and looking for something interesting to do." He stopped there, still wearing that unpleasant smile. "And some*one* interesting to do, too, I suppose. Anyway, she was just fine covering for me."

I thought of Josie's assessment of Emily Porter, that she was a flaky girl who didn't spend much time worrying about the future. Even so, you could be a total flake and still not be okay with murder. "Even after she found out Lilith was dead?"

"Yeah. I told her Lilith had been arguing with one of her fans before the ritual, and maybe that was who was responsible. And she believed me."

Of course she did, probably because it was easier to convince herself that Boden's story was the truth than to admit the man she'd brought home the night before was a stone-cold killer.

"And today...?" I prompted, knowing I needed to hear the whole story, hard as it might be. I still didn't know how in the world I was going to get myself out of this mess. A quick glance around the room didn't offer much in the way of self-defense. Too bad Emily wasn't a smoker. A heavy marble ashtray might have done the trick if I'd been able to catch Boden off guard.

At last, he let go of my wrist. The slightest pause, as if he was observing me closely and looking for any sign that I would bolt. I would've taken off like a runner from the starting block if I'd thought it would do any good.

Unfortunately, he was still standing close enough that I knew he'd be able to tackle me before I traveled a foot.

"I didn't want to," he said. "But then Doug showed up, yelling at me that the accountant had records of all the money I'd stolen, and that he was going to start an investigation as soon as he got back to Southern California. I told him he didn't know what he was talking about, that Lilith gave me access to that account so I could go shopping for her, but he still kept spouting off. Finally, he left, but the damage was done. Emily started asking all these questions, wanting to know if I was in trouble...and also if I'd killed Lilith to cover up what I'd done."

He stopped there, using both hands to run through his hair and push it away from his lean, aquiline face. If I'd passed someone on the sidewalk wearing that particular ferocious expression, I would have hurried across to the opposite side of the street, but unfortunately, I didn't have that luxury here. No, I was like someone trying to thread their way across a lava flow on a series of not-too-stable stepping stones.

"And so...?" I said, and stopped. I honestly wasn't sure whether I wanted to know what he'd done. Emily was just an innocent bystander, guilty of nothing more than some spectacularly bad judgment.

"I told her to be quiet, but she wouldn't stop asking questions. So...I made her stop."

Suddenly, I wasn't dealing with just a single chill down my back, but a sensation that felt as if someone had abruptly tossed me into a meat locker in a bikini. I didn't know if I'd ever be warm again.

"Anyway," Boden went on, as casual as though he was discussing what he'd had for breakfast, "she's handled, and I figure I can take her car. It's a pretty sweet ride, and I don't have any wheels of my own because I drove here in Lilith's car. We can go anywhere we want."

The word squeaked out before I could stop it. "'We'?"

Abruptly, his brows drew together in a fearsome scowl. "Yeah, *we*. Wasn't that the point of me telling you all this? You needed to know the truth so you'd come along with me. Well, now I've told you. And we should go. I don't think anyone's going to come sniffing around here, but better not to take the chance, right?"

"'Right,'" I echoed, even as my mind worked furiously. There had to be some way I could turn Boden's delusions to my advantage. "But I drove over, so I need to take my car home. No point in leaving it here and letting people connect the two of us, right?"

Boden frowned again, but then his expression

cleared as he nodded. "That makes sense. I can follow you and park a little ways away so it's not too obvious we're together. Then you can go get some things from your apartment."

In preparation, I supposed, for the road trip he was imagining. Maybe he was visualizing us as a modern-day Bonnie and Clyde...or as the two seriously skewed protagonists from *Natural Born Killers.*

If that was the case, then he was in for some serious disappointment. A killer I was not, and I also woefully lacked the skills necessary to hold up a convenience store.

However, I figured that getting away from Emily's house was a step in the right direction. At least in my apartment, I'd be on home ground, and could possibly come up with a strategy for incapacitating Boden Marsh. Too bad I hadn't left the crystal ball out in the living room, although I doubted I'd be able to get away with that kind of maneuver twice in a row.

"Sounds like a great idea," I said, summoning a false smile.

"Okay," he replied. "My stuff is ready, so we can head out now."

For the first time, I noticed that a black leather duffle bag sat on the floor, partially obscured by one of the couches. Obviously, he'd been planning to bug out as soon as he thought the time was right.

I wanted to curse my crummy timing. For all I knew, if I'd come over even ten minutes later, he would have already been on his way and I could've avoided this whole disaster.

But the universe had sent me to be here in this particular moment. I could only hope it knew what it was doing.

"This way," Boden said, and he led me out of the living room and into the kitchen, and then through a side door that gave access to the property's long driveway. It might've been quicker to go out the front, although this way, there was much less chance of anyone spotting us as we got into Emily's Mustang.

Which I knew was probably the point.

I sat quietly as he backed out of the driveway. "Where's your car?" he asked.

"Just down the street, behind that silver Chevy."

A nod as he scanned the street. No one seemed to be around.

"Give me your phone."

Oh, hell no. "I'm not going to call anyone—"

"Maybe you're not," he cut in. "But this way I'll know for sure."

Defeated, I dug the phone out of my purse

and handed it to him. He shifted in the car seat so he could slide it into his back pocket.

"Get out and head home. I'll follow you—and don't try anything stupid. This thing can blow the doors off your Volkswagen."

I wanted to be offended on my car's behalf... but I knew he was right. Meekly, I got out of the Mustang and headed over to the Beetle, then slid into the driver's seat. As I buckled the seatbelt, I found myself praying that one of the neighbors would emerge from their house and demand to know why Boden was driving Emily Porter's flashy new car.

But no one appeared, and I found myself letting out a resigned breath as I navigated my way back to Broad Street and the building that housed both my apartment and my store. I had to wonder what Boden would do if I suddenly veered off course and made a beeline for the police station—the Globe station, since of course, it was much closer than the headquarters for the San Ramon tribal police.

Unfortunately, I didn't possess that sort of nerve, mostly because I knew Boden Marsh was just crazy enough to rear-end me or attempt some kind of pit maneuver if I did anything out of line. While I didn't fear bodily injury on my own behalf, I definitely didn't want any innocent bystanders dragged into this whole mess.

Well, at least any more than already had been, I thought, feeling a wave of sadness at what he'd done to Emily Porter.

I parked behind the building, and Boden followed suit. Since no one else was back there, he probably had decided it was better to stick close than worry about whether anyone would see us together.

He approached as I was unlocking the back door. I didn't say anything, only went inside and let him follow me up the stairs to my apartment.

Because I'd been in such a hurry when I left, I hadn't engaged the alarm system. As soon as we were both in the apartment, I said, "This will only take a couple of minutes. Do you want a glass of water or anything while you wait?"

There…that sounded normal, didn't it?

"I'm fine," Boden replied. A jittery nervousness seemed to have overtaken him, because his fingers played with the silver skull belt buckle at his waist, and once again, he rocked back on his heels. "Just hurry…and leave your purse here."

Clearly, he was only willing to trust me so far, even though he already had my phone. I realized then what a tightrope I walked, and a spasm of fear made my throat clench. Even if Calvin had gotten my text message, he would have gone over to Emily Porter's house to find me.

And he'd be way too late.

Since I didn't know what else to do, I pulled out my overnight bag and threw a pair of jeans, a skirt, and a couple of T-shirts and tank tops inside, along with several changes of underwear. Into the *en suite* bathroom to fetch an assortment of toiletries and a hairbrush and comb, and I thought I'd amassed a collection of items that made it look as though I really was ready to go on this crazy road trip, even though I still couldn't quite believe any of this was really happening.

No sign of Archie, either. I'd noted in passing that he'd already eaten the food I set out for him, even though it wasn't quite six-thirty yet. So much for his much-vaunted dedication to a strict schedule. Most likely, he was sleeping off his meal somewhere and wouldn't even realize that anything had gone wrong until it was way too late.

I emerged into the living room, overnight bag dangling from one hand. "Ready!" I said brightly. "Which way are we headed?"

"East," Boden said. He'd brightened upon seeing the bag I held, as if somewhere in the back of his deluded mind he'd maintained one shred of sanity that told him I might not be as willing a participant in his crazy scheme as I'd pretended to be. "No one will expect us to go that way."

I had my doubts, but I knew to keep them to myself. About all I could do was hope that Calvin would be able to put the pieces together and figure out what had happened to me.

If Chief Lewis even let him. If he suspected Boden Marsh had kidnapped me from my apartment, then that crime was firmly in his jurisdiction.

I'd just opened my mouth to say driving east sounded like a great idea when a gray blur bolted out of the hallway, sped past me, and rammed right into Boden's leg as he was beginning to take a step in my direction. He stumbled, and, without thinking, I swung my overnight bag up into his jaw with all the force I could muster.

A startled "oof!" escaped his lips as he lost his balance and went down hard, his head missing one of the dining room chairs by mere inches.

Darn.

Still, I knew I didn't have a moment to lose. "Get him, Archie!" I called out, and the cat descended on my unwanted guest's face, scratching and hissing.

"*Aiee!*" screamed Boden, desperately batting at the attacking feline with both hands.

While he was occupied trying to fend off the cat, I hurried into the kitchen and got out one of my trusty extension cords, and tied it around his feet. As soon as Boden realized what I was doing, he tried to lash out at me—and actually landed a pretty good kick on one of my shins—

but I only gritted my teeth against the pain and kept going.

Soon enough, I had him pretty well hog-tied, and did my best to ignore the threats and insults he hurled my way as I pulled my phone—somehow unscathed—out of his back pocket. However, before I could even enter my passcode, someone pounded on the front door.

"Selena! Are you in there?"

Calvin. I shot Archie a grateful look and a thumbs-up, and he gave one of his patented cat shrugs and headed back down the hall toward the office. I didn't know whether he didn't want to speak around Boden—although, according to him, I was the only one who could understand what he said, thanks to being a witch—or whether he didn't feel like wasting time pointing out that once again, he'd been forced to come to my rescue.

I got to my knees and hurried over to the front door. Calvin stared down at me, looking positively wide-eyed for him.

"Are you all right?"

"I'm fine," I said, although I knew I might have to reassess that claim once I was able to determine exactly how much damage Boden's kick had caused. "Here's your guy."

I stepped out of the way so Calvin could get a

good look at our perpetrator, still squirming and cursing on the floor.

Those amused crinkles appeared around his dark eyes. "I see you've put those extension cords to good use again."

"They do come in handy," I admitted. "Although I'm starting to think I should invest in a pair of handcuffs."

A flash of white teeth. "I like the sound of that."

Exasperated, I poked him and nodded toward Boden. "First things first."

Still smiling, Calvin went and knelt next to the other man. "Boden Marsh, I'm placing you under arrest for the murder of Lilith Black. You have the right to remain silent…."

I listened, and felt a smile of my own touch my mouth.

Sometimes, justice was served piping hot.

18

All's Well

IT TURNED OUT THAT THE REASON WHY Calvin hadn't arrested Boden Marsh for Emily Porter's murder as well was because she wasn't actually dead.

After Boden had been carted away by a couple of San Ramon tribal police, headed for his arraignment, Calvin stayed behind at my apartment to fill me in.

"I got your text and went over to Emily's house right away," he explained. "When there wasn't an answer, I went ahead and broke in so I could search the place. I found her on the floor in the master bedroom, tied up and barely breathing."

"What did he do to her?" I asked, not sure if I really wanted to hear the answer.

"Strangled her and left her for dead," Calvin said. His mouth tightened in anger before he went on, "But she's a tough girl, and she hung on. If I'd been even a few minutes later...."

The words trailed off there, and I shivered, then said, "But you weren't. You got there in time."

"Barely. I called an ambulance and waited until she was taken away, then figured since you weren't at her house, you must have gone back to your place." He paused there and sent me an unreadable look. "What in the hell was Boden Marsh doing here?"

"Kidnapping me so he could take me on some sort of cross-country crime spree," I replied. "Or maybe just trying to get me away so I could become the ultimate witch of his fantasies. I don't know for sure...and I probably don't want to."

Judging by the hard, flat line of Calvin's mouth and the way his fingers clenched on the knees of his khaki uniform pants, he was less than thrilled by that answer. However, he didn't try to ask why I hadn't fought back—after all, Boden Marsh had already amply proved that he was a very dangerous man.

Good thing even he wasn't up to the challenge of facing down a cursed cat. Archie had a *lot* of anger to work off.

"The guy definitely isn't firing on all cylinders," Calvin agreed. "I'm sure they'll give him a full psych eval to determine whether he's competent to stand trial."

I wasn't sure how to feel about that. On the one hand, if Boden really was suffering from the sort of extreme psychological issues that would prevent him from understanding right from wrong, then a psychiatric care facility seemed to be the right place for him. I didn't know if that was truly the case, though. He might have been sick...or just plain evil.

Either way, I was fine with letting better minds than mine figure it out.

After Boden had been taken away, I'd made fresh cups of herbal tea for Calvin and myself. I lifted my mug and took a sip, glad of the warm liquid flowing down my throat. Even though the day was boiling hot outside, I still felt cold all over. That had been a close one. If it hadn't been for Archie....

"But," Calvin went on, "since Boden Marsh confessed his crimes to you and Emily is still alive to testify against him, he's going to have a hard time coming up with a workable defense. He'll be arraigned for the murder of Lilith Black and the attempted murder of Emily Porter, and whatever the outcome, he won't be going anywhere for a very long time."

"And that means everything will get back to normal in Globe," I replied.

"One can only hope." Calvin's dark eyes took on a glint I'd begun to recognize. "I have to say that I'm not sure things will ever be completely normal while you're around."

"You say that like it's a bad thing," I said, and he chuckled.

"Not bad. Just…different."

"In a good way?"

"A very good way."

He leaned in and kissed me, his mouth warm and welcome, tasting of vanilla tea. I fell into his embrace, glad of his arms around me, and even more glad to know that there weren't any more secrets between us.

From somewhere down the hall came an irritated huff of a breath. "Oh, dear lord," Archie groaned. "Just when I'd hoped this place had started to quiet down."

Calvin pulled away from me and looked over his shoulder toward the hallway. "Is your cat all right? It sounds like he's having a coughing fit."

I tried not to smile. So that's what Archie talking sounded like to anyone who wasn't a witch.

"Hairball," I said briefly, and leaned in for another kiss.

All right, so I might have had *one* secret left… but I'd leave that for another day.

The End

Selena's adventures will continue in *Household Demons,* releasing in July 2021.

Also by Christine Pope

HEDGEWITCH FOR HIRE

(Mystery/Paranormal romance)

Grave Mistake

Social Medium

Household Demons

Perpetual Potion

Wandering Monsters

THE WITCHES OF WHEELER PARK

(Paranormal romance)

Storm Born

Thunder Road

Winds of Change

Mind Games

A Wheeler Park Christmas

Blood Ties

Healing Hands

Wishful Thinking

Mysterious Ways

A Canyon Road Christmas

Demon Born

An Ill Wind

Higher Ground

Haunted Hearts

THE WITCHES OF CLEOPATRA HILL*

(Paranormal Romance)

Darkangel

Darknight

Darkmoon

Sympathetic Magic

Protector

Spellbound

A Cleopatra Hill Christmas

Impractical Magic

Strange Magic

The Arrangement

Defender

Bad Blood

Deep Magic

Darktide

THE DJINN WARS*

(Paranormal Romance)

Chosen

Taken

Fallen

Broken

Forsaken

Forbidden

Awoken

Illuminated

Stolen

Forgotten

Driven

Unspoken

THE WATCHERS TRILOGY*

(Paranormal Romance)

Falling Dark

Dead of Night

Rising Dawn

THE SEDONA FILES*

(Paranormal Romance)

Bad Vibrations

Desert Hearts

Angel Fire

Star Crossed

Falling Angels

Enemy Mine

TALES OF THE LATTER KINGDOMS*

(Fantasy Romance)

All Fall Down

Dragon Rose

Binding Spell

Ashes of Roses

One Thousand Nights

Threads of Gold

The Wolf of Harrow Hall

Moon Dance

The Song of the Thrush

THE GAIAN CONSORTIUM SERIES*

(Science Fiction Romance)

Beast (free prequel novella)

Blood Will Tell

Breath of Life

The Gaia Gambit

The Mandala Maneuver

The Titan Trap

The Zhore Deception

The Refugee Ruse

STANDALONE TITLES

Hearts on Fire

Taking Dictation

Golden Heart

Night Music: A Modern Reimagining of The Phantom
of the Opera

Ghost Dance: A Sequel to Gaston Leroux's The
Phantom of the Opera

Flight Before Christmas

* Indicates a completed series

About the Author

USA Today bestselling author Christine Pope has been writing stories ever since she commandeered her family's Smith-Corona typewriter back in grade school. Her work includes paranormal romance, fantasy romance, and science fiction/space opera romance. She makes her home in New Mexico.

Don't miss out on any of Christine's new releases —sign up for her newsletter today!

Christine Pope on the Web:
www.christinepope.com

www.ingramcontent.com/pod-product-compliance
Lightning Source LLC
Chambersburg PA
CBHW052021240626
47153CB00006B/1899